"Hey, McCoy, he[...] new partner."

David took one look toward the door and felt an inexplicable urge to run. Walking toward him was Kelli Hatfield—the same sexy, innocently insatiable, utterly feminine Kelli Hatfield he'd shared a bed with last night. Her face mirrored the shock he felt.

It couldn't...there was no way in hell that this...that *she*...was his new partner. The reality that this gorgeous woman was actually a cop was enough to send him reeling.

Kelli appeared to regain her bearings before he did. "Officer McCoy," she said, clearing her throat. Apparently remembering where they were, she thrust her hand—her delicate, *talented* hand—toward him.

David took it, tempted to pull her into the nearest room where they could have a little talk...and then some. He looked up to find Officer Kowalsky studying them guardedly.

"You two know each other?" he asked.

David looked into Kelli's eyes. "Yeah," he said, tempted to add, *In the biblical sense.*

Dear Reader,

Sexy as sin and impossible to forget—that's THE
MAGNIFICENT McCOY MEN! First brothers Marc,
Mitch and Jake stole our romantic hearts. Now the
youngest McCoy, David, is proving he's just as much
a McCoy as his brothers.

In *You Only Love Once*, maverick cop David McCoy
never dreams that the magnificent woman he
undresses one night will show up at the precinct
in uniform the next morning. Worse, Kelli Hatfield,
David's sexy new *partner*, is determined to prove
herself his equal—on the job *and* in his bed. Has
the precinct Casanova finally met his match?

We'd love to hear what you think of the youngest
McCoy. Write to us at: P.O. Box 12271, Toledo, OH
43612, or visit us at the Web site we share with other
Temptation authors at www.temptationauthors.com.
And be sure to keep an eye out for the next and
final book of the series, featuring stubbornly sexy
Connor McCoy, available in July.

Here's wishing you love, romance and many happy
endings.

Lori and Tony Karayianni
aka Tori Carrington

Books by Tori Carrington

HARLEQUIN TEMPTATION
716—CONSTANT CRAVING
740—LICENSE TO THRILL*
776—THE P.I. WHO LOVED HER*
789—FOR HER EYES ONLY*

*Magnificent McCoy Men

YOU ONLY LOVE ONCE
Tori Carrington

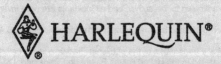

HARLEQUIN®

TORONTO • NEW YORK • LONDON
AMSTERDAM • PARIS • SYDNEY • HAMBURG
STOCKHOLM • ATHENS • TOKYO • MILAN • MADRID
PRAGUE • WARSAW • BUDAPEST • AUCKLAND

We heartily dedicate this book to romance-friendly booksellers and librarians everywhere, especially Mark Budrock, Dawn Rath, Kathy Andrico, Jim Beard, Chris Champion, Barb Kershner, Sharon Harbaugh, Kathie Freedly, Joan Adis and her lovable staff, Lisa Hamilton, Kristin Fennell, Kery Han, Betty and Fred Shultz and their partners in crime, Joan Selzer, Cathy Bartel, John Cleveland, Colleen Lehmann, Kathy Hendrickson, Heather Osborn, Lori Grassman, Judy and Bob Dewitt, Cy Korte, Michele Patrykus, Gayle Davis, Tracy Marr, Molly Carver, Rosechel Sinio, Bessie Makris, Eileen Masterson, Linda Membel, Donna Leaver, Delores Silva and last but certainly not least, Donita Lawrence.

Although we write the stories and Harlequin publishes them, it's each and every one of you who makes sure our books find their way into the readers' hands. Thank you doesn't begin to cover it.

ISBN 0-373-25923-9

YOU ONLY LOVE ONCE

Copyright © 2001 by Lori and Tony Karayianni.

1

"YOU'RE LATE."

David McCoy slid onto a stool next to his brother Connor and shrugged out of his sheepskin coat. He glanced at his bulky black sports watch as he rubbed his hands together to warm them. It was cold even for December in D.C., the kind of cold that inspired the saying, "it's too cold to snow." But the bar was pleasantly warm and decked out festively for the holiday season. Green garland laced with red lights hung behind the counter, and hurricane candle centerpieces were placed on tables around the room. He motioned for Joe, the bartender at The Pour House, to bring him a brew when he finished serving a guy down the long length of the oak bar. "Yeah. Lieutenant Kowalsky wanted to have a few words after I knocked off tonight." He greeted a couple of fellow officers taking their seats a few stools down. "Looks like I get a new partner tomorrow."

Connor knocked back what remained in his own glass. "Should be interesting."

"Yeah." David paid Joe and made a comment on the busyness of the place this early on a Thursday night. Joe shrugged and told him whatever paid the bills.

"What will this be? The third?" Connor asked as Joe took an order down the bar.

David grimaced at his older brother. Connor knew how many partners he'd gone through. He could probably recite their names, and exactly how long it had taken David to scare them off. Connor was good that way. Always the one to remember when one of them had gotten the measles, when their homework had been due and which forms he had to forge so they could participate in school-sponsored road trips. Mostly, his diligence was welcome. There were times, however, when he wished Connor would get a life—preferably, his own.

He had the sinking sensation this was going to be one of those times.

He drank more of his beer than he intended and gritted his teeth at the onset of a cold headache. Of course, in the case of his last partner, Lupe Ramirez, he hadn't exactly scared her off. In fact, she'd very nearly been killed off. A perp at a twenty-four hour convenience store had taken a potshot at her while he'd been making his way around the back. Lupe was still in rehab, learning how to walk on her reconstructed knee.

"At least the odds are against me getting another female," he said.

Connor grinned. "You sure about that? If Ramirez filled some sort of gender quota, odds are probably in favor of you getting just that."

David shook his head adamantly. "No...Kowalsky might not like me very much, but he wouldn't do that to me again. Uh-uh."

His brother shrugged. "No skin off my nose who you work with or don't. I'm just pointing out the possibilities."

"And I'm telling you the possibility isn't even remote, not even slim. In fact, the possibility is so remote, it's an impossibility."

Connor's grin grew wider.

"What?"

His brother shook his head. "Did I say anything?"

"No. You didn't have to. That stupid grin of yours says it all." David sat up and straightened his denim shirt. "Anyway, at least I do know my partner isn't fresh from the academy. He's a transfer from outside. And no matter what you say, he will be a *he*. I've done my duty as far as equality between the sexes goes. Is it too much to ask to be assigned a guy this time around?"

Connor seemed exceedingly interested in the bottles lining the wall behind the bar and took a slow sip of his beer, his grin apparently making it difficult.

David couldn't resist. He slapped his hand against his older brother's back, nearly causing him to spew the contents of his mouth all over Joe, who now stood before them putting together a purple concoction on the other side of the counter.

"So tell me, Con, what's the deal with you? Why did you want to meet here?" He held his hand up. "Wait, don't tell me, you're getting married, too, aren't you?"

Connor's expression grew darker with each question until he looked a word away from knocking David from his stool.

David held up his hands. "Hey, don't look at me that way. You're the one who called me, remember?"

"Yeah, I remember, all right. Though I'm having a hard time recalling why." He visibly winced. "Married? What on God's green earth would make you ask that?"

For some reason David had never tried to decipher, he'd always loved getting under Connor's skin. Maybe because it was so easy. Or perhaps because it was so much fun to watch Connor go from self-righteous know-it-all to a put-up-your-dukes teen in a blink of an eye. Pops had warned him that one day he'd take his banter a little too far and find himself knocked into the middle of next week. But somehow David had always known Connor would never lay a fist on him.

And, for other reasons he preferred not to pursue, he suspected it was why he'd always felt slightly separate and apart from his brothers. Too young to participate in all the older McCoy guys' reindeer games. The one to be sent to his room when discussions grew serious. Hell, he didn't even look like them, what with having blond hair and being a tad bit shorter than them all at five foot ten. And he didn't even have the benefit of a red, glowing nose so he could prove to them that he was up to the task of leading them through a foggy night—or any task, for that matter.

He shrugged. "Why not marriage? Seems like everyone else is getting hitched these days. Why should you be any different?" He knew the quickest route to pissing Connor off was mentioning him and marriage in the same breath, and he'd done it not once, but twice. His brother had been miserable during Thanksgiving dinner at the McCoy house three weeks ago. Grumbled comments ranging from "all these damn women running around the place" to "you've all turned into a bunch of wusses" encompassed the whole of Connor's contributions to any ongoing conversation.

David braced himself for another Connorism as his brother scowled. "What was it you said to Mel when she asked when *you* were going to settle down? When Satan takes up snow skiing?"

Connor's grin made a comeback. "Yeah. Well, that's about the time I get anywhere near an altar, too."

David leisurely watched a woman in tight jeans walk by, then turned back toward his beer and his brother. "So why did you call then?"

"Does there have to be a reason?"

He watched the way Connor shifted on his stool. Yeah, he'd say his brother had something on his mind, something heavy. "With you, uh-huh. There definitely has to be a reason." He took a long pull from his own bottle. "Come on, Con, just spill it, will you? You've never been the kind of guy for a boys' night out drinking. Actually, you were always telling the rest of us when it was time to lay off the stuff. So what gives?"

Connor grimaced. "I don't know. It's just this thing with Pops...."

David waited for him to continue...and waited...and waited.

"Man, you're about as talkative as Jake tonight. You know, if you really want this to begin resembling a conversation, you're going to have to start with finishing your sentences. I'm no mind reader."

Connor leaned back and released a long-suffering sigh. "Look, this isn't easy for me, you know? You guys are usually the ones coming to me for advice."

"Yeah, it must really eat you that you're stuck with me."

Connor looked at him, a question in his blue-green eyes. "Is that what you think?"

David was the one who shifted in his seat this time. "Come on, Con, quit pussyfooting around and get to the point already, will you?"

"It's just...aw, hell, David, do you think I did the right thing with Pops? You know, telling him I didn't approve of his going out with Melanie's mother?"

David remembered the incident at the cemetery. His brows shot up. "Didn't approve? You practically told the old man you'd disown him if he didn't stop seeing Wilhemenia." He motioned for Joe to bring Connor a fresh bottle. "Have you two even spoken a civil word to each other since then?"

His brother looked away.

"You haven't, have you?" He rubbed his chin, thinking of the times the family had gathered together over the past couple months. He couldn't come up with a single time when he'd seen Connor and Pops talk to each other. Oh, yeah, Connor may have mumbled a jab or two under his breath, but he'd never directly spoken to their father. "Out of all of us, you were always the closest to Pops. I don't know if it's an age thing..." Connor gave him a glowering look. "Sorry. What I'm trying to say is that if two men ever understood each other, it was you and Pops."

"Yeah, well, I guess this Wilhemenia stuff really got to me, you know? Thanks." He grabbed the bottle Joe put in front of him. "Of all the women Pops could have chosen, why did it have to be that sourpuss excuse for a human being?"

David's burst of laughter died down. He thoughtfully rolled

his beer bottle between his palms. "I don't know what you're looking for here, Connor, but if it's reinforcements, you're looking in the wrong place. I, for one, don't happen to see anything wrong with Pops getting a little—"

Connor whipped up his hand to stop him. "Don't. What I'm interested in finding out is how you would feel about him...well, actually bringing her into the family."

David thought that if his eyes had widened any farther, his eyeballs would have splashed into the bottle he was just about to press to his lips. "You mean, like *marry* her?"

A shadow of a smile played around Connor's mouth. "See, it bothers you, too."

David put his bottle down on the bar. "I wouldn't say that, exactly."

"So what would you say...exactly?"

"I...I don't know." He looked at his brother. "Do you think it's that serious?"

Connor sighed. "I don't know. Right now, no. I think after...our little talk, Pops did stop seeing her. But it's only natural to think that he was serious about her. I mean, it's not like Pops has ever dated before."

David frowned. "Wait a minute here. If he's not seeing her anymore, then what in the hell are you worried about?"

Connor fell silent, staring at his bottle as if a genie would appear any moment and supply him with the answer. "It's just that...I don't know. Pops looks so..."

"Miserable?" David grinned at Connor's quick glare. "Hey, I'm capable of noticing some things, too. And Pops is definitely miserable."

"Yeah, well, he'll get over it."

"If that's how you really feel, then why are we talking about it?"

Connor looked at him as if he was surprised by the realization. "I don't know."

A wink of neon pink distracted David. He turned to watch

the tantalizing back of a woman walking toward the pool tables. The pink of her top clung to slender shoulders and a narrow waist before giving way to form-fitting black slacks designed to drive a man wild. She met another woman, then picked up a pool stick, flicking her silky blonde, shoulder-length hair over a sculpted shoulder. David got a good look at her face. Heart-shaped. Large green eyes. A bow-shaped pink, pink mouth. Everything about her seemed delicate in some way. Utterly, totally feminine. Innocent. So unlike most of the women he typically dated.

His gaze drifted lower. Whoa. There was nothing innocent about the way that top fit. The curve-hugging material outlined her breasts perfectly, and hid very little—like the fact that she was either cold or tuned in and turned on by his slow visual examination.

He groaned deep in his throat. He managed to croak out a response to Connor. "Yeah, well, you might want to try figuring out the answer to that question before you go on to the next." His gaze again strayed to the pool table.

Damn, but she's more woman than any two men could handle, David thought as she returned his measuring gaze. A smile turned up the sides of her mouth and he came close to letting loose a long, appreciative whistle. Despite the fact that they were in a cop bar, there was no way this woman was one. Nor was she a cop groupie like the table of women nearby who consistently went to cop bars pretending to be out for nothing more than a good time, but were really angling for a wedding ring.

No. This woman was neither. She probably did something...womanly. Sold wedding dresses, worked in an antique shop, sold perfume at an upscale department store. She probably wouldn't know how to hold a gun, much less fire one. The thought was altogether appealing. Especially since he didn't plan to repeat the mistake of sleeping with someone on the force again.

He cleared his throat, then slanted a loaded gaze his brother's way. "Speaking of the weather, I think I just heard that Hell's forecast calls for a blizzard." He pushed from his stool as if compelled by a force greater than himself. "I just spotted me the woman I'm gonna marry."

"Who was talking about the..." Connor's spine snapped military straight as he apparently realized what was going on. "Aw, hell, David, I didn't come over here to watch you play Casanova."

"You can have the friend," he said, straightening his shoulders.

"Gee thanks, but no thanks."

"We're done, here, right? All we're doing is talking in circles anyway. Come on. Let's see if we can go get in on some of this action."

Connor hiked a skeptical brow.

"I'm talking about pool, doofus. What did you think I meant?"

"I don't play pool."

David barely heard him, his gaze fastened on the woman even now bending over to set up her next shot. Her toffee-colored hair swept down over her face and, with cleanly manicured nails, she pushed it so the strands mingled with the hair on the other side of her perfect head. Her gaze shifting back to him, she pulled the pool stick back then scratched, completely missing the ball. She might not know much about the game of pool, but she'd look damn hot stretched across the green felt...naked as the day she was born.

"Look out, here he goes again," he overheard a fellow officer say to another as he walked by them, the comment punctuated by laughter.

David's grin merely widened.

"IF THE DEVIL wore jeans, this is what he'd look like."

Kelli Hatfield laughed at her friend's whispered comment,

then self-consciously tugged the snug, unfamiliar pink material of her new top away from her skin. She didn't have to ask who Bronte was talking about. The blond guy from the end of the bar, who could easily have posed for Michelangelo's *David*, was sauntering their way. And saunter was about the word for it. With his sexy gaze openly fastened on her, he gave the impression that she might be his destination. She swallowed hard, straightened, then resisted the urge to pluck at her top again. She caught her friend's cautionary gaze but purposefully ignored it. The same way she had ignored Bronte's groan earlier when she saw what she was wearing. And her arguments when Kelli had suggested they go to the renowned D.C. cop bar for "just one drink and a game of pool." And her warnings that she was just looking for trouble by shimmying like that when she bent over to take a shot. Until that moment, Kelli hadn't known she *could* shimmy.

A delicious, reckless shiver glided down her spine.

Bronte leaned closer. "Don't even think about it, Kell. The guy's Grade-A trouble. In capital letters. Bolded. Underlined. A lady-killer and a half."

Kelli's smile widened as she brushed off her friend's warning. When was the last time she had felt this way? Keyed up? Sexy? Ready to take on the world? Well, okay, maybe not the world, but certainly the prime male specimen heading her way. She frowned slightly, not knowing what was worse— the fact that she couldn't remember the last time she'd felt this way, or the suspicion that she never had. The unclear answer made her all the more determined to pay attention to the fiery emotions.

Sure, she admitted it probably wasn't very wise to openly encourage a guy in a cop bar, considering her circumstances. But it was her first night living in D.C. after three long years. And, by God, it felt good to be home, in the city where she'd been raised and where she planned to live out the rest of her life. It felt good thinking about her new job and knowing she had a choice apartment in Columbia Heights, the equivalent of which she would never have been able to afford in New York City. Overall, she felt good. And the instant she'd exchanged glances with the man now close enough for her to see the color of his eyes—a warm, vivid blue that sent another shiver sliding behind the other—she'd felt the overwhelming need to cut loose in a way she never had.

"Tonight, maybe Grade-A trouble is what I'm in the market for," Kelli said, enjoying her friend's shocked expression.

There wasn't much capable of shocking Bronte O'Brien. If she were to be honest, Bronte had always been the shocker out of the two of them. Ever since forming an odd union of sorts while taking pre-law at George Washington University, Bronte had been the racy one, reckless, the girl on scholarship who hid her brains behind her good looks. Kelli had lived vicariously through her best friend for years, though she had to admit Bronte's life had become boring as of late. Still, it was long past time Kelli started doing her own living.

Bronte rubbed the smooth skin between her brows and sighed. "You know, Kelli, I take back everything I've ever encouraged you to do. For years, I've been telling you that you need to loosen up. Get out and experience life. *Get* a life." She slowly shook her head, the dim light burnishing her short red hair. "But this is definitely *not* what I had in mind. If you won't take the advice from me, personally, take it from your trusted attorney—you don't want to do this. I know the guy he's with—I've run across him on the job. He's a marshal. Anyway, a guy like this one making a beeline for you...well, he has catastrophe written all over him. He should come with a warning label—Commitment Phobic— Use For One-Night Stand Only."

"You're not my attorney, Bronte. You're a U.S. attorney. And I'm not interested in his friend. I'm interested in him."

Kelli looked her full in the face. "Besides, maybe a one-night stand is all *I'm* looking for."

"That's what you say now. Let's see how fast that story changes afterward."

Kelli leaned against her stick. "Come on, Bron, lighten up. You're acting like my sleeping with this guy is a forgone conclusion." She held up a rigid finger. "One. That's the whole of my experience with the opposite sex." An experience she didn't want to repeat much less remember. "Only then I was so green you could have planted me."

"So you say. Mark my words, Jed was an amateur. This one's a pro." Bronte hooked a thumb to where the guy in question stopped to talk to a couple of men at the bar, though his gaze never strayed from their direction. "A regular heartache waiting to happen."

Kelli rolled her eyes to stare at the ceiling, then laughed. "Why don't you let me be the judge of that?" She drew her thumb along the smooth wood of the pool stick then bit softly on her bottom lip. "Come on, Bronte, I'm tired of being a good girl. Fed up with always doing the right thing, both in my job and my personal life. The perfect worker who passes up a vacation day because a coworker needs to go to his kid's school play. The friend who's always home because she never goes anywhere, never does anything. The boring neighbor who doesn't mind feeding your pets while you're away sipping Bahama Mamas on some tropical island. I want to step outside my safe little box, live a little, even if just for this one night."

Kelli swallowed, not understanding the scope of her restlessness until that very moment. There had been hints over the past few months. The Egyptian silk sheets she'd dropped a fortune on because she thought they were sexy. Her new interest in cooking exotic foods; she'd even bought a wok, for God's sake. Her sudden, insatiable hunger for romance novels, addictive books she had only picked up on occasion before, but now her collection had grown so large it had taken five huge boxes to cart it from New York. The simple truth was that she no longer wanted to rub her legs against the sheets...alone. She didn't want to spend hours concocting the perfect meal only to be disappointed when she discovered she and her dog Kojak were the only ones around to eat it. She wanted to *live* the lives of those romance heroines rather than just read about them.

"And as for your worrying about me getting my heart broken," she continued, "give me a little credit, will you? I think I deserve at least that after all the heartaches I watched you experience. I never said word one to you all those times you got yourself in trouble over some walking stud muffin."

"What, are you actually inventorying each of my doomed romances so you can be sure to get in all your I told you so's?" Bronte grimaced and held up her hand. "And don't try to give me that innocent look either." Her blue eyes twinkled as she sipped her purple drink. "Just how do you think I learned how to give you a hard time now?"

Kelli squinted at her.

"Every little jab I've just hit you with, you've poked at me over the years."

Touché. She leaned over the table and lined up her next shot. Right before she would take it, she glanced past the cue ball and directly into the suggestive eyes of the man in question. She scratched so badly she nearly tore a hole in the green felt.

The guy grinned and began swaggering their way again.

Bronte dropped her voice. "Just don't say I didn't tell you so, you hear?"

Kelli didn't absorb her friend's words, concentrating instead on the heat spilling through her bloodstream, the tingly tightening of her breasts. Tonight she wanted to be the ravisher *and* the ravishee. She wanted to throw her hands up in the air and say "I am woman, hear me roar." And she wanted to swallow the gorgeous guy moving toward them whole.

Shamelessly she openly eyed the man's physique. Oh, he was a cop all right. There was no denying that. Everything about him spoke of cockiness and authority, a rough-around-the-edges attitude that stemmed as much from knowing himself capable of saving someone's life as from the certainty that he could take a suspect's. And he was still young enough to think himself immortal.

She briefly caught her bottom lip between her teeth again. Maybe he was just the thing this good girl needed to turn very, very bad.

He reached the pool table just as someone finished feeding the jukebox a slew of coins. Bronte rolled her eyes as Bob Seger's "Night Moves" attempted to drown out the hum of conversation and clink of glasses from behind the bar.

The devil in blue jeans slapped a fiver on the edge of the pool table near the coin slot. "I play the loser." His grin made her heart race. "David McCoy."

Kelli repositioned her pool stick and slowly shook his hand, the heat the simple touch generated exhilaratingly cathartic. "Kelli Hatfield." She released his hand then tapped the stick lightly against her side. This was one game she was going to enjoy losing. "You're on."

TWO HOURS LATER, David launched a renewed assault on Kelli Hatfield's luscious mouth and backed her toward her stripped bed in the corner. Her hungry but obviously inexperienced response made him harder than steel. As drop-dead sexy as the woman was, an innocence clung to her silky skin like an irresistible perfume, making him want to breathe her in, eat her alive, thrust into her like nobody's business.

And that's exactly what he intended to do. That is, if he could pull his thoughts together long enough to take things further than kissing.

The strength of his reaction was like a sucker punch to the gut. Even he had to admit surprise at how quickly they'd ended up back at her place, clawing at each other's clothes, devouring each other's mouths. He'd lay ten-to-one odds that the woman even now clumsily unzipping his fly had never uttered the words "one-night stand" before, much less indulged in one. Still, he hadn't had to resort to any of his old come-on lines at the bar. It had always been a bit tricky trying to get a woman between the sheets while keeping her well away from serious commitment territory. After their sexually charged game of pool, he'd simply suggested they get out of there, and she'd agreed. Even Connor and her friend, Bronte, had held up their hands as if their leaving were inevitable and said little more than "Bye" when they grabbed their coats and practically ran from the bar.

Just thinking about the remarkable, lightning-fast string of events sent David's pulse rate skyrocketing off the charts. Hell, he felt he might lose it if he couldn't bury himself in her hot flesh right then and there.

He supposed she might be drunk, but he knew what signs to look for and she displayed none of them. In fact, he didn't detect a hint of liquor. Rather, he tasted something hot and undeniably sweet on her tongue. Then there was her skin....

Peaches. She tasted like peaches, for crying out loud.

Off went that stretchy pink top and her lacy bra. He palmed her breasts and groaned at their nicely rounded weight. Not too big. Not too small. Pure heaven.

"Wait...I..." she whispered huskily.

He pulled an engorged, pale nipple into the depths of his mouth. She gasped and ceased trying to speak.

With more strength than he would have thought possible, she reversed their positions then pushed him toward the mattress. Off went her slacks, his jeans. Before he knew it, his fingers were entangled in her hair, his mouth greedily pulling at hers, and she was poised, ready, above him.

He tugged his mouth from hers and met her eyes. In the fleeting beams of passing headlights, he saw on her face a gravity, a need, a beauty that made him groan. He'd experienced one or two one-night stands in the past, but this was different somehow. Rather, Kelli Hatfield was different. He'd never felt so in tune with a woman, so completely wrapped up in her. And though they didn't know each other well, he felt that he *knew* her on a level that transcended the trivial details normally exchanged during the traditional first few dates. He didn't know what college she had attended in New York, where she'd said she just moved from, but he knew that she wanted him as much as he wanted her. And that was saying a whole lot.

Her gaze remaining locked with his, Kelli lowered herself. His hips bucked and suddenly her tight, slick flesh surrounded him.

He recaptured her mouth and closed his eyes, feeling an odd sensation of inner calm even as their movements grew restless, their breathing ragged. When they climaxed together minutes later, he felt an odd sense of completion that stemmed from more than just the physical. The sensation was foreign, frightening, electrifying, and completely blew his mind.

"Wow," Kelli whispered, her damp flesh resting against his.

"Yeah...wow," he repeated.

Slowly, his breathing evened, his heartbeat went back to normal, and the world came back into focus. He glanced around the room. Boxes everywhere. There weren't even sheets on the bed, though the old radiator in the corner emanated so much heat, it didn't matter. He vaguely wondered if she'd just moved in, but didn't have the energy to ask. For the first time since he could remember, David McCoy was completely devoid of words.

She rolled off of him and reached for a robe pooled on the bare wood floor. He fought the urge to pull her back.

"I could do with a glass of something cold. How about you?" she asked, tucking her tousled hair behind her ear.

David noticed the way she didn't look directly at him, rather concentrated on a spot just over his right shoulder. His brows shot up. He recognized her actions all too well, because, simply, he was usually the one who made them after sex. He pushed himself up onto his elbows. God, this was a first. "I...yeah, sure. I could go for some water or something."

A whole holding tank full of ice-cold water, he thought.

Tying the robe around her trim waist, she scooped up the empty condom packet from the nightstand, then padded barefoot from the room.

David lay still for a long moment staring after her. So that was it, huh? The most explosive sex he'd had...well, that he'd ever had, and it was over. It was time for him to leave.

He closed his eyes and groaned. Mitch had always warned him that one day he'd pay for his errant ways. He absently scratched his head, the thought of one brother leading to thoughts of another. Was Connor somewhere getting better acquainted with Kelli's friend, Bronte, right now? Or had he taken off right after he and Kelli had?

For the life of him, he didn't want to move. He wasn't sure what exactly had happened just now. The sex between him and Kelli was...well, whatever it was, he had to get himself some more of that.

Something cold and wet nudged against his foot. David went from complete relaxation to nearly catapulting from the bed at Olympic record-setting speed. He thoroughly searched the area but found nothing on the quilted blue-flowered mattress. If that was a bug, it had to be one of the slimiest...

There was a click-click against the wood floor. David

looked anxiously around the room for something to defend himself with. He settled on one of his hiking boots. He slowly moved toward the end of the bed aided only by the boot and the dim light filtering in through the window. Not only did it have to be the slimiest, it must be the biggest damn bug—

A hulking, jowl-drooping blond boxer stuck his head out from around the corner of the bed and eyed him, his tongue seeming to curve upward toward his nose. David sagged with relief. A dog. It was a dog. Sensing that the crisis had passed, the ugly pooch came loping around the corner, his wagging short tail making his entire overly plump body shimmy.

David reached down to let the canine sniff the back of his free hand. "Hey..." he craned to see, "boy. How are you doing, huh?" He heartily rubbed him behind the ears.

A switch clicked, then an overhead light filled the room with its harsh glare. David blinked rapidly to adjust his eyesight, then looked at where Kelli stood in the doorway, a brow raised in question. David grimaced at his undressed state and the hiking boot he still held. *Way to go, McCoy.* It began to sink in that he wasn't going to be getting anymore of anything anytime soon.

WOW.

The word ran through Kelli's mind like a hit compact disc on permanent replay, despite the strange scene she encountered when she returned to her bedroom.

Her brain had effectively stopped working, oh, about an hour and a half ago at the bar, when she'd basically decided she was going to take one delectable David McCoy home with her. And it hadn't switched on again until she found herself lying on top of David, gloriously sweaty, wondering what in the world had just happened.

Despite her arguments to Bronte to the contrary, the limited scope of her experience had left her criminally unprepared for this man and her phenomenal reaction to him. She pulled her white, threadbare robe more tightly around herself with one hand. If this was what made Bronte jump into every bed she came across, then she herself had definitely been missing out on a whole lot of something for much too long.

The only problem was that remembering how very bad she'd just been made the good girl come out to do some mental finger-shaking.

The boot David held clunked to the floor and he grinned boyishly. "Uh...your dog and I were just getting acquainted."

Dog... Oh, God, her dog! "Kojak! Come here, boy." She'd purposely closed the bedroom door when they'd come in, but the pooch must have snuck in while she was in the other room. "There you are."

"I thought he was a bug."

"What?"

David was tugging up his jeans, his back to her, his firm, rounded behind tempting her touch. She averted her gaze and felt her cheeks color—which was ridiculous, because mere moments before she'd shamelessly run her fingers all over the flesh in question. "Never mind."

"I have your water," she blurted needlessly, the plastic glass in her hand.

Clad only in jeans, he sauntered over to her and accepted the cold drink. While he drank, Kelli covertly skimmed the well-toned body she had hungrily molested in the dark and was shocked by the rush of desire to consume him all over again. She mimicked his movements by swallowing hard. The guy was perfect in every sense of the word. His abs stood out in wondrous relief, making her itch to run her fingers over the sculpted muscles, down to where a thin line of blond hair disappeared into the waistband of his jeans.

"So that's it then, huh?" he asked, holding out the glass to her.

Kelli took it. "Did you want more?"

The odd way he looked at her made her rethink her question. "Depends on what you're referring to."

Kelli's cheeks burned hotly all over again. He wasn't talking about water. He was likely referring to the fact that she hadn't given them the chance for more. After they'd...had sex, she couldn't have run from the room quicker had it been on fire.

The dog butted his head against her shin, then ran around her legs in an attempt to gain her attention. "Not now...Jack."

David's grin nearly knocked her over. "Good thing you clarified who you were talking to, 'cause I was just about to grab my shirt."

Bronte would be happy to know that every last thing she'd uttered about David McCoy was absolutely, positively, one hundred percent true. He was a pro. And now that Kelli's head was working again, she was beginning to fear she was greener now than she'd ever been. Beginning to fear that it was impossible for her to have casual sex, because tomorrow kept intruding, making her wonder about stupid things like whether or not he would call her, or if he liked Chinese food.

Her gaze drifted down the sculpted planes of his chest and her own breathing grew curiously ragged. Green or not, she still wanted this man with every fiber of her being. She looked at his flat, beaded nipples and her own tightened and ached to be touched. She saw the thick ridge pressing against the zipper of his jeans, and felt a rush of hot desire between her bare legs.

She flicked her eyes up to stare into his, recognizing and instantly responding to the need reflected in the midnight blue depths. The hungry, sex-deprived wanton may have abandoned her, but she was finding that the good girl wanted everything she had...and more.

A tiny whimper gathered in her throat. Oh, to hell with to-morrow and consequences and hearing Bronte say "I told you so." The simple truth was that it was still night, and she wanted to spend every single last moment of it with David McCoy cradled between her thighs.

Forgetting the dog, she practically leapt on David, circling her arms around his neck, pasting her mouth against his and hungrily letting him know exactly what she was feeling. He slid his hands inside her robe and the ineffective belt slid to the floor...right along with the empty plastic glass. David grinned then scooped her up and practically tossed her back on top of the bed.

2

"YOU'RE LATE, Officer McCoy. Again."

David waved away O'Leary, the desk sergeant, and his penchant for protocol as he rushed by on his way to the briefing room. He'd run into bumper-to-bumper traffic near Dupont Circle, so had parked his car in the station commander's spot in front of the street level building to save time. His uniform shirt was wrinkled because when he'd looked for it on the passenger's seat—where he thought he'd put it when he leapt into the car half-dressed—he found instead that he'd been sitting on it. And he hadn't had a chance to clean and check his firearm, as he did every morning.

Despite all that, he caught himself whistling.

Okay, so it was tuneless, and he was also pretty sure he looked like Gomer Pyle on drugs, but he couldn't help himself.

Slowing his step, he made sure the back of his shirt was tucked in, folded his police issue winter jacket over his arm, and started to turn the corner. Lieutenant Kowalsky would have his ass for being late again. Still, suffering through old Kow's impending wrath didn't bother him half as much as it normally would. His good humor might have something to do with last night, and the incredible mind-blowing sex he'd had with Kelli Hatfield.

Kelli Hatfield.

If it was true what they said about the whole Hatfield and McCoy feud...well, then, he and Kelli had made it their duty to put a huge dent into righting old wrongs.

"Nobody's in there."

O'Leary's words reached him the instant David opened the door to find the briefing room empty. He relaxed his shoulders from their stiff at-attention angle then glanced at his watch. Certainly, he hadn't missed roll call.

"Okay, O'L, what gives?" David stalked back to the front desk.

"Didn't have your radio on during the drive in, did you, kid? Everyone's downtown. Some guy's holding his little girl hostage until he can talk to his estranged wife. The whole city and county forces are down there now, not to mention every branch of the news media."

David felt the familiar, all-powerful burst of adrenaline kicking in. A hostage situation. Now that was a meaty way to start a day. He sprinted for the door, shrugging into his coat as he went.

"McCoy!"

David winced at Kowalsky's shout. He'd recognize that low, eardrum-popping sound anywhere. The guys around the station joked that you could hear his voice in the next county if you listened hard enough.

"Yes, Lieutenant?" he said, turning to face him, though he maintained his momentum.

"Going somewhere?" Kow asked, eyeing his shirt and raising a brow.

David either had to go through the door or stop. Given the warning written all over his superior's face, he opted for stop. "Yes, sir, I thought I'd head downtown to see if I could be of assistance."

"Aren't you forgetting something?"

"Sir?" Methodically, he patted his badge, his firearm, his cuffs. All there.

"Your new partner, McCoy. I'm talking about your new partner."

David winced for the second time. That's all he needed. A new guy to play getting-to-know-you with during the ride downtown. He quickly rebounded. "Sorry, sir. I'd assumed that since I was late, he would already be on the scene."

Contrary to his name, Kowalsky was a six foot five African-American with the manner of a drill sergeant and a monstrous grin he used only to his advantage. That he grinned now made David mutter a mild oath.

"What was that, McCoy?"

"Nothing, sir. My new partner... Where can I find him?"

Kow's grin widened. "Right here, McCoy."

He turned to find the hall empty. The grin left his face. "Hatfield!"

The bottom of David's stomach dropped out. *Hatfield.* His mind quickly calculated the odds that he would meet two Hatfields in less than twenty-four hours. They were very small. So small as to be minuscule. So tiny as to be impossible...

Naw. He had Hatfield on the brain, that's all.

He made the mistake of looking at Kow's suspicious grin, noting the telling absence of his new partner—as if he or *she* didn't want to be seen—and felt the sudden, irresistible urge to run. Especially when the sweetly sexy, innocently insatiable, utterly feminine Kelli Hatfield popped out from around the corner, her face mirroring the shock he felt.

Forget his stomach. The floor had just dropped out from beneath his feet.

It couldn't...wouldn't...there was no way in hell that this...that *she*...was his new partner. Hell, last night he judged her competence to be somewhere between squirting perfume on little blue-haired ladies with platinum credit cards and helping panicky brides try on their wedding dresses. The reality that she was actually a cop was enough to send any man reeling.

Kelli appeared to regain her bearings before he did. "Officer McCoy," she said, clearing her throat. Apparently remembering their company, she moved her coat from her right to her left arm, then thrust her hand—her soft, slender, *delicate* hand—toward him.

David took it, tempted to use it to pull her into the nearest room so they could have a little talk. *Now.* Kow be damned.

Speaking of Kow, he glanced to find him staring at them guardedly. "You two know each other?"

David nearly choked on the words, "yep, in the most sinful sense."

"Yes, sir," Kelli answered instead. "We met last night at The Pour House. First night back in town, as luck would have it."

"Good." Kow nodded. "Now isn't there some place you guys need to be?"

He had to be dreaming. That was it. This was all some sort of sick, twisted nightmare brought on by what happened to his ex-partner and his anxiety of who his new partner would be. At any moment he would—

"McCoy!" Kow barked. "Get with the program, man."

David winced. If this was a dream, what the hell was Kowalsky doing here?

Kelli gave him a pointed look. "We're on our way, sir," she said.

Completely dumbfounded, David watched her walk by him. Catching a whiff of her subtle scent didn't help matters any. His gaze zipped around the station lobby, but he didn't find any chuckling officers hiding behind any doors or around the corner. O'Leary wasn't even watching them. And Kow's expression darkened further with each second that passed.

This is for real. It wasn't some really bad practical joke being played on him by fellow, prankster officers. Kelli Hatfield truly was his new partner.

Yeah, and he was the king of Siam.

Picking up his jaw off the gritty tile, David hurried after Kelli's trim little bottom. The door closed after them and he stopped again. After a few steps, she turned toward him, shrugging into her coat. "Are you coming, McCoy?"

"There's no way...I mean, I don't believe... Come on, Kelli, you *can't* be a police officer," he blurted.

She planted her fists on her hips, her expression altogether thunderous. "Which one's ours?"

"Huh?"

"The car, Officer. Which is our vehicle?"

David pointed left to the cruiser in the lot and watched her head for it. She reached the driver's side. The impact of what her actions meant provided the impetus he needed to finally move. He was next to her in no time flat. "I'll drive."

Rolling her eyes toward the sky, she took her hand off the handle, then rounded the car and got in the passenger's side.

David stood still for a long moment, concentrating on little more than his breathing. This couldn't be happening. Any second now he expected to wake up from this dream—*nightmare*—and find his mind was playing some sort of sick joke on him after last night's recklessness. He bent over and looked through the window. Kelli was fastening her seat belt. He snapped upright again. Nope. She was still there.

Damn.

KELLI SAT flagpole straight, staring at the dash like a dazed crash victim waiting for the airbag to deflate. Her friend Bronte's words of warning from the night before echoed in her mind. "Just don't say I didn't tell you so...."

Somehow she didn't think this was what Bronte had in mind. Though her friend would probably argue it was exactly what she deserved—right after she laughed herself into hysteria.

Kelli closed her eyes tightly. Only to her. This could happen only to her. Her first night back home in D.C., the one and only night out of her entire life that she had thrown caution to the wind, and she wound up spending it with her new partner, screwing up both her personal and her professional life.

She scrubbed her damp palms against the scratchy material

of her police issue slacks and whispered a long line of curses that would have done her police chief father proud. Well, it would have done him proud if, indeed, she'd ended up being the son he'd wanted instead of his only daughter. But she hadn't, and it was a fact he never let her forget. Not when she'd played little league baseball. Not when she'd enrolled in the academy at twenty. Not when she'd graduated and was denied a spot with the D.C. Metropolitan Police. It hadn't helped any when she learned that her father made sure her status was knocked down to third tier standby, essentially barring her from a job on the force. Apparently he had thought she would lose interest in her pursuit while in the academy. He'd always been so overprotective. As he'd told her, no little girl of his was going to get her butt shot off so long as he had any power within the department. And as Regional Assistant Chief for the East, he had more than enough to waylay her...at least in D.C. In New York, however, his power was nil.

The driver's door finally opened and Kelli nearly launched from her seat. David slid behind the wheel. She pointedly avoided his gaze and suspected he did the same beside her.

He's just as much a victim in this as I am, she reminded herself. But for some reason his undisguised disbelief when they were introduced irritated her. Shock, she expected. Disbelief? Suddenly agitated, she shifted. She told herself to give him the benefit of the doubt. That there was a good chance he wasn't like eighty percent of the other males she'd worked with who thought her completely incapable of her job as a police officer. Okay, maybe not a good chance. But there was a chance. And after last night, she, um, owed him at least that much consideration.

He moved. She forced herself to look at him. His mouth was moving, but no words made it past his impossibly wicked lips. She swallowed, reminding herself that she wasn't supposed to notice what a great mouth he had...or remember all the naughty places that mouth had been mere hours earlier.

His attempts at speech continued, nudging up her impatience level. Finally, she said, "Look, I didn't expect this anymore than you did, David...um, McCoy." *Stick to last names.* Maybe that would afford her the distance she so desperately needed right now.

His crack at imitating a wide-mouth bass out of water stopped and he seemed to relax. "Actually, Hatfield," he said, stressing her last name. "That's not entirely true. Last night *you* knew you were going to be reporting to work at *this* station and that you would be assigned a *new* partner. That's a helluva lot more than I was privy to."

She sighed and stared at the ceiling of the car. Okay, she'd give him that. Still... "Come on, David, we met at a cop bar. Surely you had to know there was some connection."

"All right. Sure. Maybe. But as someone's daughter. Or sister. Or..."

She raised a brow, daring him to say "cop groupie."

He cursed under his breath. "I didn't expect you to be a blasted police officer."

She stared out the windshield as a couple of uniforms walked by, openly curious about the couple in the squad car a few feet away. "Don't you think we should get going?"

"Huh?" He followed her line of vision. His long-suffering sigh told her he'd somewhat snapped out of his momentary trance.

"Look, David, when I came in this morning, this was the last thing I expected." She hated that she noticed his eyes were an even more vibrant blue in the light of day. "I say we do this. Go on about our business for now and pretend last night never happened."

He blinked as if the effort took every ounce of his concentration. "Are you crazy?" he said, startling her with his intensity. "I have the best friggin' sex of my life and you tell me to forget about it? Act like it never happened?"

Heat spread quickly through Kelli's veins, making her remember just how incredible last night had been for her, too. But last night was last night. And, oh boy, did the guy who sang "What a Difference a Day Makes" ever know what he was talking about.

David started the cruiser and began to back out. "Ain't a chance in hell I'm going to forget about last night, Kelli." He looked at her. "And I'll be damned if I'm going to let you forget either."

THEY ARRIVED on the scene to find the street glutted with blue-and-whites. David spotted the scene commander and within moments he and Kelli were next to him. A brisk December breeze brought her scent to him. Damn, but she smelled good. Like ripe peaches picked fresh from the tree.

He grimaced. Yeah, she was a peach all right. A peach with a gun.

"Glad you could join us, McCoy," Sutherland said dryly.

An officer David recognized as being at the bar the night before chuckled as he elbowed his partner.

"Look, loverboy has himself a new partner."

"Can it, Jennings," David told him. His gaze rested on Kelli's face to find bright spots of red high on her cheeks. But whether her flush was a result of the cold, or the obvious gossiping going on, he couldn't tell. Her shoulder-length toffee-colored hair was caught back in a neat French braid, her skin nearly flawless where the gray morning light caught it.

She looked at him. He immediately looked back at the commander. "Why don't you bring me...us up to speed on what's going on?"

Sutherland did, covering much the same ground O'Leary had at the station. Except his details were more specific. The perp was on the third floor. Door was open, but there wasn't a clean shot. He pointed to where the perpetrator's estranged wife stood shivering next to a nearby patrol car, then to a fire escape on the side of the building. Across the way on the roof of a neighboring building a couple of sharpshooters were setting up shop.

"The perp demands to talk to his wife before he'll give up the three-year-old girl."

"The perp is the child's father?"

"He ceased being a father the minute he took his own child hostage, McCoy."

David stepped backward until the fire escape was in sight, ignoring the red-and-white flashes of light against the brick building.

"What is it?" Kelli asked, coming to stand next to him.

He looked at her again. Damn, but just looking at her did all sorts of funny things to his stomach. "Just that the guy couldn't have picked a worse time to do this, that's all. You've got the tired third shifters exhausted and pumped up on caffeine, their trigger fingers itchy as hell. Then there are the first shift guys barely awake and pissed as hell that their coffee-and-donut run was interrupted." He grimaced. "Really bad timing."

Her gaze swept him from forehead to mouth. Was she remembering last night as vividly as he was? Was she thinking about how great it had felt to be joined together, far, far away from this mess? She looked quickly away and this time he was sure the color of her cheeks wasn't due to the cold. "Any ideas on how to end it?" she asked.

He mulled over her words. "Yeah. I think what I just said makes a lot of sense."

"What, let SWAT take him out?"

"No. The donuts part. If the father's just coming off third shift he probably hasn't had breakfast yet. A guy can get awful hungry after putting in a full one."

"Are you saying we should feed the perp?" she asked, a suspicious shadow darkening her green eyes.

"The father, Hatfield. The guy is the kid's father." He grinned. "And yeah, I think we should try feeding him." He shrugged. "Couldn't hurt."

He scanned the street. At the corner was a small donut shop. He thrust five dollars at her. "Here. Get a half dozen and a couple of coffees."

Kelli frowned. "But—"

"Do it, Hatfield."

Her eyes flashed, but she started toward the shop—though not without looking back a couple of times first.

The instant she was out of sight, David grabbed a bulletproof vest from the back of a riot wagon, then strode toward the fire escape. He pulled down the ladder even as he shrugged into the vest. He pulled his weight up on the first rung, then methodically climbed until he reached the third floor landing. Ducking off to the side, he peeked in through the window. The father was sitting on a couch out of view of the front door and of the sharpshooters across the street, grasping his little girl in one hand, a twelve-gauge shotgun in his other. The little girl looked unharmed. More than that, the toddler didn't seem to have the slightest idea that things were out of control as she giggled and toyed with the buttons down the front of her father's work shirt.

David ducked back out of sight and took a deep breath. He figured out the scenario in his mind. The father had just knocked off work at a nearby factory, had stopped by to see his daughter, his soon-to-be ex refused to allow him to, and he'd taken matters into his own hands.

Any way you cut it, what had begun as a harmless domestic squabble had spiraled out of control until you had the situation he now faced.

"I've got a clean shot," a sharpshooter's voice crackled over the radio fastened to David's gun belt.

"Be at the ready," scene commander Sutherland's voice responded.

Shaking his head, David reached over and tested the old wood-frame window. Unlocked. Hoping the bit of luck would stay with him, he pushed the window up before the guy inside, and the commander outside, had time to react.

"Whoa, there, cowboy," David said, swinging his feet over the sill and sitting with his hands up. "My name's McCoy and I'm here to make sure no one gets hurt." He grinned. "Especially me."

OFFICERS, uniformed and otherwise swarmed the small, neat apartment, talking into radios, issuing orders and generally making a mess out of things. In the middle of the chaos, Kelli finished reading the perp his Miranda rights, then cuffed him. Distractedly, her gaze trailed over to where David stood near the door holding the little girl. She clung to him like a young chimp. He leaned in and whispered something into her ear, then chucked her under her dimpled chin. She twirled her blond, sleep-tousled hair around her chubby index finger, then giggled shyly. Somehow, David had not only skillfully managed to keep the girl from seeing her father being arrested, he had made her laugh. Kelli couldn't help noticing how...right he looked holding the little cherub.

Testing the cuffs, she forced the unwanted thought aside and concentrated instead on her total lack of amusement only moments before. David's sending her off on some two-bit, phony errand so that he could play maverick hero set her blood to simmering.

"This way," she said, grasping the perp's elbow, then angling him toward the door.

He hesitated. "I didn't mean for any of this to happen. I just wanted my face to be one of the first she saw this morning, that's all," he told her. "It's her birthday, you know. All I wanted was five minutes to give her a hug and her present. I would never have hurt my little girl."

Kelli took in his aggrieved expression. "I hope not. But that's for a judge to decide, isn't it?"

David handed the child off to another female officer who

would likely take the toddler to her mother and Kelli passed the handcuffed perp off to the first officer on the scene.

"That was a stupid stunt you pulled, David," Kelli muttered as they walked out of the apartment together.

"Just so long as it's over and no one got hurt." He acknowledged a hearty slap on the back from one of their colleagues with a nod. He flashed a loaded grin at her. "I didn't know you were so concerned about my backside."

"I'm your partner," she said, her breath catching at the teasing expression on his face. "I'm supposed to be concerned about your backside. But that's not what I was talking about. I didn't much care for your little diversionary tactic, David. Do you even know the definition of the word partn—"

"McCoy! Get your ass over here now, boy," Sutherland's voice boomed up the stairwell.

"Speaking of backsides..." David groaned. "I'd better go see what he wants."

Kelli opened her mouth, then snapped it closed again. She got the impression that whatever she had to say wouldn't make one iota of difference anyway.

She stopped and let him pass in front of her. "Go ahead. I just might enjoy watching the scene commander take a piece out of you."

David's grimace was altogether too cute. "Be careful what you wish for, Hatfield. At this rate, I won't have any behind left to risk." He waggled his brows.

Sutherland was at the bottom of the steps and was apparently ready to do just as David forecasted. Even so, Kelli couldn't help eyeing the backside in question. The clinging, unattractive material and bulky weapons belt was unable to hide the fact that David McCoy's behind was the stuff of which fantasies were made. She started to push wisps of hair from her forehead only to find her hand shaking. She greeted an officer, then outside on the street away from the crowd she took a deep, calming breath.

Why did she get the feeling that everything in her life had just been turned upside down? And why was it that she suspected that a certain precinct Casanova named David McCoy was solely to blame?

3

THE FOLLOWING MORNING, Kelli caught herself daydreaming as she stood in front of the toaster. She'd been thinking about David in a way that had nothing to do with the way he'd treated her yesterday, nothing to do with her plans to nab a detective's shield, and everything to do with hot flesh and cool sheets.

Sighing in a mixture of wistfulness and frustration, she pushed her run-dampened hair from her cheek, then stuck half an onion bagel smothered with grape jelly between her teeth. Ignoring the dirty dishes stacked in the sink, and the empty carton of orange juice on the counter, she clutched her full coffee cup, then elbowed open the kitchen door. She had forty-five minutes before roll call. Plenty of time to peel off her sweats, catch a shower and get down to the district three station to have that little talk she and David had never really gotten around to yesterday.

The tension she had just spent a half an hour and three miles running off settled solidly back between her shoulder blades.

After the hostage case and Sutherland, there had been the press to deal with. She remembered how David's easy grin and easygoing personality had transferred well over all forms of media and felt her stomach tighten along with her shoulders. Reporters, especially female—although she'd noticed a couple of males responding to David's charming, daredevil ways— were all over him. When they'd *finally* gotten back to their squad car, it seemed a quarter of D.C.'s population had a crisis of some sort that needed attention. She and David had spent the day on back-to-back runs ranging from the simple—helping find an elderly woman's "stolen" social security check in a neighbor's mailbox—to the complicated—an obvious gang member who would probably lose an eye but would never give up the names of his homies or the opposing gang.

Still, no matter how many calls came in, how much paperwork they had to fill out, a thread of awareness had bound her and David together. It was a connection not even her sharpest retort could hope to cut.

Yeah, well, today she planned to take a machete to work. She'd get a handle on her runaway hormones if it was the last thing she ever did.

Kelli wove her way through the maze that was currently her apartment into the dining area of her living room. She dodged precariously stacked, half-unpacked boxes, a hundred pound bag of diet dog food and her treadmill. Finally she nudged a manila folder aside with her mug, then put her coffee on the cluttered dining room table. Her attention catching on a pink message slip, she freed the bagel from between her teeth and took an absent bite. The message must have slipped from one of the files, the blue ink nearly faded. She leaned closer to see the date. March 25, 1982. The day her mother was murdered. The day she'd decided she wanted to be a homicide detective.

A sharp bark made her jump.

"Yikes, Kojak, you just about gave me a coronary." Frowning down at the drooling blond boxer she'd rescued from a New York animal shelter, she considered the disgusting concoction that served as her breakfast then held it out to him. He sniffed, licked, then whined and walked away.

Kelli stared at the now inedible bagel half. "Thanks a lot." She tossed it into a nearby bag she hoped was empty, then switched on the television across the room with the remote. The local news broadcaster's voice filled the apartment reminding her again how David had charmed the reporters. His too handsome mug had been plastered all over the news last night, every hour on the hour, if not on the news itself, then in the news previews. "You don't want to miss our story of the day as local man in blue David McCoy saves the day...."

It was enough to make a person ill.

Kelli plucked up the remote again, moving to switch off the television before the news could launch into another "local hero" bit featuring her partner the sexist cad, when a completely different scene stopped her. *"We're on the outskirts of Georgetown where a woman was found dead in her apartment, earlier this morning. Eyewitnesses tell us the murder of this quiet, private school teacher bears all the markings of the work of the man dubbed the D.C. Degenerate."* The female spot reporter looked over her shoulder.

Kelli wryly nodded. "Zoom in on the standard body shot," she said under her breath.

The reporter looked back at the camera. *"If so, then I, for one, think we need to upgrade his name to D.C. Executioner. Because it appears he's just lost interest in playing out sick sexual fantasies and has just graduated to full-fledged killer."*

Kelli pressed the mute button, the case too similar to another for her comfort. She picked up the message slip lying on the table in front of her, wondering how much detectives knew about this latest guy. And if they would do any better catching him than they had her mother's killer.

It had been awhile since she'd reviewed the contents of the folders strewn out before her. Three years, in fact. Ever since transferring to New York where doing any footwork on the case would have been impossible. She sat down and curled her right leg under her. Now that she was back home, though...

The telephone chirped. Propping a file open with one hand, she reached for the cordless with her other.

"Yeah?"

"Jaysus, Kelli, is that the way you answer the phone?" her father asked with obvious exasperation.

Kelli closed the file and reached for another. "I don't know, Dad, you'd be the better one to answer that question since you are the one who's calling me every five minutes since I got back in town."

She winced the moment the words were out of her mouth. Not because she shouldn't have said such a thing to her own father, but because of what it would ultimately lead to.

She closed her eyes and waited for the inevitable speech.

"Yes, well, I wouldn't have to call you if you were staying here, now would I?"

"No, Dad, you wouldn't," she said almost by rote.

"You know I have more than enough room for you. There's no sense in your going off and getting an apartment."

"Yes, Dad, I know."

The sound of crumpling paper caught her attention. She turned to find Kojak nosing around in the bag for the uneaten bagel.

"Have you watched the news lately? It isn't safe for a woman to be living on her own in this city."

Kelli nodded. "Not safe."

"And that damn mutt of yours is no kind of security either, if that's what you're thinking. He's nothing but an overgrown cat."

"Cat..."

"Kelli Marie, are you even paying attention to what I'm saying, girl?"

"Sure, Dad. Though I really don't have to because you've said it so often it's etched in my brain." She pulled another file in front of her and flipped it open. "Was there a specific reason you called, Dad? Or is this just another of your check-ins?"

Silence, then, "Can't a dad simply want to talk to his daughter?"

Kelli slowly spread her hand out palm down on the table. She should have seen that one coming as well but stepped right through the open barn door all the same. Her voice was decidedly more subdued when she said, "Of course you can, Dad." She leaned back in her chair. Sometimes it seemed it had always been just her and her father. "You and me against the world," he'd said when he'd found her crying in her mother's closet after the funeral. Words he'd repeated time and again after she'd gotten knocked down over and over while proving to everyone and to herself that she was just as good as the guys. "It's just you and me against the world, kid."

She curled the fingers of her free hand into a loose fist. "Dad...I know it makes you uncomfortable to talk about it...and Lord knows I've avoided bringing the topic up enough times...but I have to know." She took a deep breath that did nothing to calm her. "Does it ever bother you that Mom's killer was never caught?"

She regretted the question the instant it was out. The silence that wafted over the line was as palpable as her own unsteady heartbeat. "You know I don't like talking about the past, Kelli."

"I know, but—"

"What's done is done. Nothing can change it."

I can change it. "But don't you think sometimes that it can be changed? That by—"

"No."

She bit her tongue to stop herself from asking anymore questions, no matter how much she wanted to. She knew from experience that she would only upset her father more. And the more upset he got, the more he clammed up, locking himself away even from her. She didn't want to make that happen. Not in her first few days back home, no matter how desperately she needed answers.

"Okay, Dad. We don't have to talk about it if you don't want to."

She switched the phone to her other ear, focusing her entire attention on lightening the conversation, coaxing it back to safer ground. "So tell me, big bad police chief...did you go for the Café Vienna or the French Vanilla this morning?"

For the next ten minutes she and her father talked about everything and nothing, with Kelli carefully redirecting the conversation whenever it moved too near career territory...too close to family issues that might include mention of her mother. It was altogether easier for both of them to forget that she was a police officer. Um, edit that. It was infinitely easier to make her father forget she was a police officer, much less why she had chosen the career to begin with. She wasn't sure what he told everyone about her time in New York, but if she knew Garth Hatfield, and she did, it probably had something to do with art school.

Of course that explanation would not only raise some brows now that she was back in town, it would call into question his mental capacity.

Kelli glanced at her watch. "I gotta run, Dad."

"Oh. Sure. Okay."

She methodically closed each of the files in front of her and piled them back up, chucking any idea she had of going through them this morning. "I'll talk to you later, then?"

"Later."

"Goodbye." She started to get up and nearly tripped over where Kojak was licking a jelly stain from the wood floor.

"Hold up a second, Kell." Her father's voice stopped her from hitting the disconnect button. "There's something I wanted to ask you."

She absently watched the muted images slide across the television screen. Stories of murder and corruption, all against the background of the most powerful capital of the world. Never a dull moment. "What is it?"

"How did it go yesterday?"

Kelli paused, wondering at the neutral sound of her father's voice. She decided to play it as vaguely as he was. "It went well. Really well." *Liar.* Although she was sure her dad would approve of her trouble with David even less than the idea of her putting on a uniform every morning.

"You meet your new partner yet?" he asked.

She slowly reached out and switched the television off. "Yes."

"Are you getting on well?"

Kelli crossed her free arm over her chest. "Yes."

Her father's sigh burst over the line. "Come on, girl, this isn't an official interrogation. You can give more than a yes or no answer. Do you like the guy or don't you? Do you want me to have you assigned somewhere else? Another district station, maybe?"

"Like out in Arlington where the most serious crime is loitering? No, Dad, but thanks just the same." She rubbed her forehead. So much for avoidance measures. "And my partner's name's McCoy. He's a pigheaded, male chauvinist who needs an ego adjustment, but I can handle him." At least she hoped she could.

There was a heartbeat of a pause. Kelli fought the desire to ask him if he was still there.

"McCoy?" he finally said gruffly.

"Yeah. David. Do you know him?"

"Of him. I know his father."

"That's nice, Dad. Maybe you and he can get together and plot how to scare your kids off the force over a beer sometime. Look, I've—"

"If Sean McCoy and I ever end up in the same room together where there's beer, I'd just as soon crack a bottle over his head," her father said vehemently.

Kelli's mouth dropped open. She'd never heard him say such a thing about another person. Yes, he was quite adamant on where he stood on her decisions, but that was different. In almost every other aspect of his life he was as open-minded as they came. "Dad...I don't quite know what to say. I'm...shocked."

"Yeah, well, you wouldn't be if you knew the guy. They don't make them any cockier than Sean McCoy."

He hadn't met David yet. "When's the last time you spoke to this...Sean?"

He mumbled something she couldn't quite make out.

"What was that?"

"Twenty years."

Kelli smacked her hand against her forehead. "Gee, and here I thought it was something a little more recent. Like yesterday."

"It was. I might not speak to the old geezer, but I see him just about every day on the job."

"Wait, don't tell me. He's on the force, too. What is he? Regional Assistant Chief for the West or something?"

"Chief?" Garth nearly shouted. "Hell, Kelli, aren't you getting the drift of anything I'm saying? The guy's a damn beat cop. Always has been, always will be."

"So?" she said carefully. "Look, Dad, call me slow, but I'm not getting this. What is this, a modern day replaying of the old Hatfields and McCoys thing?" She glanced at her watch and nearly gasped. "I gotta run, Dad. We can talk about this later, okay?"

She pressed the disconnect button while he was still blathering on. She cringed. No doubt she would hear about *that* later, as well.

DAVID STARED at his watch for the third time, although no more than a minute had passed since the last time he'd looked. The briefing room was already filled to capacity. Which wasn't abnormal in and of itself, except the collection of plainclothes at the front of the room had ignited gossip among the officers surrounding him.

Where is she?

"What do you think's up?" Jones, next to him, asked.

David shrugged. "Beats me."

"Harris thinks it's the Degenerate case."

He grimaced. "All this attention for a sexual deviant? Seems a little excessive."

"Where you been, man? The guy's been promoted. He's chalked up his first killing. Body was found this morning, though they think she's been dead a couple of days."

David recalled the case. "Damn."

Jones chuckled. "You got that right."

"Did I miss anything?"

David looked to his left where Kelli had claimed the seat he'd been saving for her. She looked far too fresh, too alert, for first thing in the morning. And far too enticing. It was all he could do not to pant all over her like a Chihuahua, bug eyes and all.

"You're late," he said, unhappy with the simile. A Chihuahua? He should be something more manly, like a German shepherd at least.

And Kelli was one hundred percent groomed white poodle, pink bow and all.

She smiled. "Yes, I am, aren't I?"

It took David a full second to realize she was referring to her lateness, not to his mental comparison.

She shifted her weight so that she could slip his notepad out from under her curved bottom. "This yours?"

David snatched it away, telling himself the paper couldn't possibly be warm after so brief a contact.

"Did I miss anything?" she asked again.

David crossed his arms, tempted to ignore her. After her dumping maneuvers yesterday after they kicked off work, he'd spent the entire night at his father's place glowering...and watching Pop glower, too. Not a fun way to pass the time. "It's about the Degenerate case."

Her eyes lit up. "You mean the D.C. Executioner case now, don't you?"

"You know?"

"Of course I know. Don't you watch the news, McCoy?"

He wanted to tell her that no, he got enough of real life on the job, but he didn't think it would reflect well on him. So instead he said nothing, because to imply that he usually did watch the news, but had missed it now, might hint at a break in his routine. Which might then lead to her assumption that she was the cause for this disruption. He wouldn't in a million years let her think that. No matter how on the mark the assumption would be.

Instead, he grinned. "I, um, had other things to do last night."

The light extinguished. "The news came through this morning."

David shrugged. "Same difference."

Kelli sat back in her seat and sighed. "Please, do spare me the details."

He leaned in a little closer, eyeing the clean stretch of flesh just below her ear. "Oh, I don't know. I was hoping you and I could, um, go over them blow-by-blow. Say tonight? Over dinner?"

He never saw her fist coming, but he had no doubt that's what hit him in the arm. "Ow," he said, rubbing the sore spot.

"Come on to me again on the job and you'll be hurting a lot worse than that, McCoy. Now stop your whining. They're about to start."

And start they did. But David only listened with half an ear about the formation of a special task force headed up by homicide in cooperation with the Sex Crimes unit. They were looking for a few good men and women to go undercover. SC already had three detectives working undercover at three different sex shops across the city that the earlier victims may have frequented. They needed another.

David couldn't care less. His academy test scores had all basically come up with "does not play well with others." It was exactly the reason he'd been through three partners in less than seven years. Even if he had a mind to apply for a position on the task force—and he didn't—they'd probably laugh him out of the interview.

Still, it wasn't his lack of interest in the goings-on that worried him. Rather, his intense interest in the woman next to him.

Why had she dodged his attempts to get her alone last night? One minute he'd been shooting the breeze with a couple of other officers back here at the station, the next he'd turned around to find her gone.

He'd thought about showing up at her place unannounced with a six-pack. And probably would have had she been anyone else. But for some reason the thought of her shutting the door in his face had chased him out to Pops's instead.

Was it his imagination, or had the sex between them the other night been as good as he remembered? And if that was the case, why was it that Kelli looked like she'd rather be anyplace else on earth than sitting next to him?

Unless...

Oh, God, he couldn't even bear to think that he'd somehow fallen short of the mark performance-wise. Missed the three-pointer. Left her swinging in the proverbial wind.

He shifted and covertly eyed her. Naw. It wasn't even remotely possible that lady-killer David McCoy had left a woman sexually unsatisfied. Hell, he had a black book full of names to prove differently. An endless list of women just begging for a phone call from him.

He crossed his arms. It wasn't possible.

He slanted her another glance. Was it?

"That's it. If anyone has any questions, feel free to ask the detectives here. We should be getting a suspect sketch out to all units before the end of first shift." A pause. "And officers, I won't kid you. We don't know what we're dealing with here, what the suspect's capable of and how far he intends to go. The female officer who signs on will be faced with a very dangerous situation. We want you to take that into consideration before tendering your name."

David practically sprang from his chair. "Thank God, that's over. You ready?"

Kelli grimaced. "I've got...something to do first. Meet me out at the car?"

He shrugged. "No prob."

Women. Probably had to go powder her nose or something. Lord forbid she should look less than her best to apprehend a shoplifter.

KELLI DISCREETLY wiped her sweaty palms down the length of her slacks when she finally left the briefing room. Her chances of winning the grand prize in the Publisher's Clearinghouse sweepstakes were probably better than getting on that task force. She'd only been on the job in D.C. for two days. What did it matter that she had three years of solid experience in New York? Or that she'd gone undercover twice there as a prostitute to arrest potential johns?

Still, she'd had to submit her name for consideration, no matter what the outcome. Chasing down men who preyed on women was exactly what she'd always been driven to do. If she couldn't find closure in her mother's case, she could make damn sure no other young girl had to face what she had. She would offer them closure. A chance to see the offender punished for what he'd done to a loved one. An opportunity to go on with life knowing that there was some justice in the world.

She had to do it. No matter how dangerous the road she had to take to get there.

She shrugged into her coat and opened the outer door, admitting that maybe her chances at the assignment were better than she thought. Even she was surprised to find the task force already had her personnel file. Written there in black and white for the entire world to see was her career goal: become a full-fledged homicide detective before she reached thirty. She cringed. Sure, that was her goal. But what had she been thinking when she wrote that little tidbit down for her supervisors to see? She might as well have written that when she was ten she'd wanted to be president of the United States.

"Smooth move, Hatfield," she muttered to herself as she put on her hat.

She wasn't surprised to find David glowering in the squad car, tapping the face of his watch like a taskmaster. Kelli climbed into the passenger's side, inclined to tell him that she had enough on her hands with one father, she didn't need another. But that might lead to her revealing who her father was, and she wasn't quite up to dealing with that can of worms right now.

"Took you long enough," he said, backing out. "What did you do, eat some bad Chinese or something last night?"

Kelli stared at him, her mouth agape. Of course he would think she'd needed to make a pit stop at the bathroom. She wouldn't be surprised if he thought she'd needed to powder her nose, or whatever men thought women did nowadays. Lord forbid she'd have any interest in joining the task force. And far be it from her to fill him in. It would only make it worse when she found out she hadn't made it.

She snapped her mouth shut. "Yeah, something like that." She switched on the radio and picked up the handset. "Dispatch, this is Five-Two, heading out." She settled back into her seat. "Look, David, you and I *really* need to have that talk I mentioned yesterday."

"About what?"

His blank expression told her he truly didn't have a clue. "About the little stunt you pulled yesterday morning."

He didn't look enlightened.

"When you sent me out for donuts while you, by your lonesome, went out and saved the world."

"Oh, that," he said, grinning. "I didn't save the world, Kelli. Just kept a guy who needed some sleep from mucking up his life any more than he already had."

"Did it ever cross your mind to consult with me first? To work out a plan together, then have Sutherland approve it?"

He appeared to think her question through, then shook his head. "Nope."

She pointed her finger in his direction. "That's exactly the reason we need to talk. Just what did you think you were doing climbing that fire escape without backup? Without anyone knowing just what you were doing? Then barging through that open window like...like some uniformed supercop there to save the day?"

He arched a brow. "Uniformed supercop?"

Kelli bit her tongue. She'd picked up the description from one of the many news reports the night before.

"Look, Hatfield, you and I could argue about this all day...and all night," a decidedly suggestive twinkle entered his eyes, "but when all is said and done, there was no time to plan. SWAT had a shot and Sutherland was about to give the order for them to take it. I had to act, and I had to act fast." He stopped at a red light. "Okay, I admit, sending you to get donuts was a pretty rotten thing to do—"

"Downright crappy."

He grinned. "Yeah. But, hell, I was still shocked to find you were on the force, much less my partner, and I needed some time to adjust before going out and playing Butch Cassidy and the Sundance Kid, you know?"

His explanation made Kelli more agitated. Only because it made a twisted sort of sense. What was the world coming to when she understood the inner workings of a mind like David's?

Worse yet, what was with her desire to keep looking at the way the material of his slacks clung to his hunky, well-defined thighs?

"Just don't do it again, McCoy, or else you won't have to worry about Sutherland taking a piece out of your behind. I'll be the one with that honor."

He flashed that devil-may-care grin at her again, making her want to smack her forehead against the dash in exasperation. "Sounds fun."

She mumbled a series of unflattering remarks under her breath.

David's grin vanished. "That was just a joke. Hey, if it makes you feel any better, I'll let you take the lead on the next call that comes in, okay? Whatever it is—bank robbery, car chase, shoplifter. You name it, I'll stand back and let you handle it any way you want to. You'll be completely, totally, in charge."

Naughty images that had nothing to do with police work slid through her mind. Finally, she managed to say, "I don't want to be the leader, McCoy. I just want to be your partner." She uncrossed her arms and smiled. "But you've got a deal."

Just then, the radio crackled. The dispatcher named a code and a location. "All officers in the vicinity, please respond."

Kelli rolled her eyes. A domestic dispute. It figured. The one call she was going to get to control and it would probably be settling an argument over who left the cap off the toothpaste.

"Aren't you going to call it in, Hatfield? We're only two blocks away," David said, then laughed so hard he had to slow down the car.

Kelli glared at him. "I was thinking about letting another patrol get it." Then she sighed and picked up the handset. "Dispatch, this is Five-Two. We've got it. ETA five minutes."

4

BOY, SHE'S EVEN more beautiful all worked up. David slipped his nightstick into his weapons belt, then closed his car door. On the other side, Kelli did the same, the high color on her cheeks reflecting how she felt. And he knew it was in response to him. He inwardly grinned. She might act like being around him didn't affect her one way or another, but her sparkling green eyes told him differently. He'd be the first to admit that having her pissed at him wouldn't be his first choice in responses, but hey, he'd take it over her pretended indifference any day.

They stood on the curb looking at the four-story, low-rent walk-up. Nothing out of the ordinary jumped out at him. Windows were closed against the December cold. A man in his thirties was leading a bicycle from the door and carrying it down the ten or so cement steps.

"So..." David began. "Lead on."

And Kelli did. Catching the door before it had time to close after the cyclist, she switched on her shoulder radio to let dispatch know where they were. No elevator. Nimbly, she climbed the interior steps to the third floor, then crossed to the door farthest to the left. Slipping her nightstick out, she rapped on the door.

Footsteps, then a voice called out, "Who's there?"

"Police. We got a call reporting a disturbance."

David noticed that she didn't say "sir" or "ma'am" likely because he couldn't identify the sex of the person inside either.

"Who?"

Kelli looked at him. "Metropolitan P.D.," she said louder.

"I didn't call any poh-leece."

David stepped down the hall and switched on his radio. "Dispatch, the resident said there was no call made."

"My records show there was. Right from the apartment in question. Do you want back up?"

Very curious. David told the dispatcher to stand by, then rejoined Kelli at the door. She nodded, indicating she'd heard.

Kelli rapped lightly on the door again. "Someone did call, *ma'am*," she said with raised brows. David shrugged. She had a fifty percent chance of getting the sex right. "Could you please open the door?"

"But I'm not dressed."

"We'll give you a few moments to put something on, ma'am. But we're going to have to insist that you open the door."

There was no mistaking the long-suffering sigh on the other side of the wood. "Okay. Just a minute."

The sound of another voice filtered through the door, then there was an ominous thump. David slipped his stick out as well. What was going on here?

Abruptly, the door opened. Kelli held her ground, but David took a protective step back. His position allowed him a better view of just how enormous the woman in the apartment was. And he guessed that she was a woman, given the brightly colored flower-print...dress she had on.

The resident filled the entire length and width of the door. In fact, she would probably have to turn sideways in order to get out of it. Kelli tossed him a nervous glance over her shoulder. Talk about David and Goliath....

"Ain't nobody make no call from here," the woman said. "I've opened the door. So you gonna leave now?"

David heard Kelli swallow. "Step away from the door, ma'am."

"Why? Ain't nothing here to see but me."

"I'm afraid I'm going to have to insist," Kelli said.

The resident held her ground. "You got a search warrant?"

"The phone call was all the warrant we need, ma'am."

"I done already tol' you—"

"Help."

David stepped up at the muffled sound of the voice emanating from somewhere behind the woman.

"I told you to shut up," the woman said, turning just enough so that they could see the person who had made the weak plea.

David heard Kelli's gasp and nearly had to put his hand to his mouth to stop his own burst of shocked laughter.

Kneeling in the middle of the living room floor was a man about a quarter the size of the woman in front of them, his skinny ribs clearly visible through the flaps of a fluorescent pink robe edged in red feathers.

"Please help me," he repeated.

"If there's no one else here, who's this, ma'am?" Kelli asked, elbowing David when his laughter threatened to spill over.

The woman hooked a beefy thumb toward the man. "That's my boyfriend, Ethan."

It took all kinds, David thought as he slid his stick back into his belt.

"You mind explaining what's going on here?" Kelli asked, obviously preferring to hold onto her stick.

"She took my clothes," the man whined.

"Took...your...clothes," Kelli repeated carefully.

The guy crawled a couple of steps closer on his knees, allowing them a peek at the pink mules he wore on his bony feet. David couldn't help himself. He made it halfway down the hall before he burst out laughing. Kelli shot him a reprimanding look, though her eyes gave away just how close she was to losing it.

She turned back to the woman. "Ma'am, would you care to explain why you took his clothes?"

"I sure would. The no-good, dirty rotten bastard stole twenty dollars out of my wallet, that's why. I told him the last time he took something from me that if he did it again, I'd make him pay." She crossed her arms over her chest. "Well, all he had to pay with was his clothes."

Kelli motioned to the pitiful looking man. "And what he has on...now?"

"Them's my things."

"Uh-huh." Kelli tucked her stick under her arm and flipped open her notepad. She took both their names. "Do you two reside here together, Mrs. Smith?"

"You can bet your narrow little behind that he don't live with me. He's lucky I even let him visit."

"Okay. What did you do with Mr. Watson's clothes?"

"I burned 'em."

Kelli's eyes widened. "You burned them?"

"I surely did. Put them in the bathtub and squirted lighter fluid all over 'em, I did. Then I flicked a match." She snapped her fingers, then hooked a thumb over her shoulder again. "That's when Mr. Shady decided to borrow some of my things."

"I see," Kelli said slowly. She eyed the situation in front of her again, then looked back at David. He shrugged. "Do you want to press charges, Mr. Watson?"

"Press charges? Against me? What about my twenty?" Betty Smith whipped it out and waved it back and forth.

"Well, ma'am, since it looks like you've recovered your property, what remains in question is Mr. Watson's property, which, of course, can no longer be recovered."

"Not to mention whatever dignity the guy had left," David murmured into Kelli's ear.

She cracked a smile, then cleared her throat. "Mr. Watson?"

Apparently sensing that things were moving in his favor, the man finally got up. David wished he hadn't. He watched Kelli cringe, then look the other way as the robe gaped open and revealed that Mrs. Smith had indeed stripped him to the skin.

"Please cover yourself, Mr. Watson."

"Oh." He quickly did as asked. "I suppose I don't want to press charges, officers. Am I free to go?"

Kelli nodded. "Yes, sir, I'd say you are."

He rushed for the door, stumbling in the mules he wore.

"You ain't goin' anywhere wearin' my stuff!"

Kelli extended her stick, preventing Mrs. Smith from grabbing Mr. Watson. "He can't leave here wearing nothing, ma'am. He'd be breaking the indecent exposure laws."

She snorted. "You can say that again. Ain't a damn thing decent about his sorry ass."

David burst out laughing again. Kelli looked about ready to beam him over the head with her stick.

Kelli turned back to Mr. Watson. "Promise you'll bring... No, scratch that. Promise you'll mail Mrs. Smith's things back to her."

"I promise."

Then he darted between them and stumbled down the hall.

"And make sure you keep that robe closed," Kelli called after him.

"I ABOUT DIED LAUGHING when he got up with all of his...um, privates just a flapping in the wind," David said, grinning.

Kelli winced. "Did you have to remind me? I could have done without that little peep show, thank you very much."

"Little being the operative word."

Despite her best intentions, Kelli sat back in the diner booth and gave into the laugh tickling the back of her throat. Her eyes began watering. Not from the piles of onions on her hot dog, but rather from the effort it took not to completely give herself over to the hysterics that threatened. It was a relief to release the tension accumulated during the long, busy morning. It was a blessing to release the tension of a whole other nature that had been building between her and her, um, partner. Sitting across from him and dishing like partners after an emotionally trying morning helped to dispel the awkwardness. Over the years she'd come to see that these little chats with fellow officers were just as important to her sanity as knowing her partner was a capable backup. Given her history—however brief—with David, she was afraid that they'd lost all ability to objectively converse as two coworkers.

He grinned and took a hefty bite of his own chili dog.

Kelli took a long, thoughtful swallow of soda. She looked around the interior of the diner, just now noticing there wasn't another officer in sight. Considering she'd left today's choice of lunch spots up to David—her own choice of Thai food the previous day a major mistake—she was surprised he even knew of any places outside the perimeter of the station, much less one that didn't include at least a dozen macho pals. The diner wasn't only private, it was...nice.

She put the drink straw in her mouth again, watching him closely. "You know that call could have turned out very differently."

His gaze skated away from where it was locked onto her mouth and on up to her eyes. "Don't I know it." He grinned. "Mrs. Smith could have given us a peep show too, which neither one of us would have soon forgotten."

She smiled and picked up her hot dog. "I'm serious." She took a bite, then swallowed. "I learned really quick that the fastest route to a disability pension was accepting situations at face value."

"In New York?"

She nodded. "Yeah. First day on the job. Or night, rather, since I started on third shift. Anyway, my partner and I were sent out on a domestic disturbance call. By the time we showed up at the place, all was quiet. The wife answered the door and assured us that everything was fine. Her husband had come home drunk and they'd had a little argument, but that he had since fallen asleep."

Apparently picking up on the seriousness of her tone, David's chewing slowed.

Kelli shrugged. "We had no reason to dispute her story. There were beer bottles littering the floor, the television was running full blast, and there was a kid in a diaper sitting on the floor by his father's feet, you know, where he was passed out on a recliner." She gave a tiny shudder, remembering the scene. "Both of us put our sticks away and were about to sign off on the case when something caught my attention."

"Ah, the rookie sees all."

She gave him a wry smile. "Something like that. Anyway, I decided that I wanted a closer look. I went into the living room and tried to prod the husband awake. Nothing. I gave him a more insistent poke and he slumped over...to reveal that he'd been shot in the back of the head. He hadn't been sleeping. He was dead. And the gun? The wife had put the toddler on top of it, still loaded, the safety off."

"Ouch."

Kelli sighed. "Yeah. Not exactly a banner first day. I had nightmares for weeks afterward."

"The first corpse is never easy," he said.

She studied his striking face then gave a small smile. "Somehow I can't imagine you having a hard time with anything."

"Are you kidding?" he said seriously, putting his hot dog

down. "I'm going to be having nightmares about Mr. Watson for the next month, at least."

She picked up a fry and tossed it at him. "Very funny."

He plucked it from his shirtfront and popped it into his grinning mouth.

Kelli forced her gaze away from him, finding him far too attractive for her own well-being. "I'm serious. Aren't there times when this job, you know, really gets to you? Makes you wonder why you ever signed up?"

David took another huge bite of his dog, then sat back, appearing to think it over. Finally, he shook his head. "Nope."

"You would say that."

"So tell me," he said, putting fries into his mouth two at a time and talking with his mouth full, "what does your family think of you being a cop?"

"I prefer police officer." She took a bite of her own dog.

"You would."

She wiped her mouth with a napkin. "There's just my father and me. And, well, to say he doesn't think much of my being a police officer would be a major understatement." She found herself unable to meet David's gaze for fear of what she would give away.

"He still in New York?"

She shook her head. "No. I'm originally from here. How about you? How does your family feel?" she asked, hoping to switch the conversational spotlight over to him for fear that she would end up just throwing her hands up and say, "Okay, my father's a police chief and why does he hate your father anyway?" She'd never been much good at deception. Except when it came to the little white lies she told herself.

Ignoring his napkin, he brushed his hands together. "Well, let's see. There are my four brothers. They couldn't care one way or another if I was a cop or not. You see, each of them is or was in law enforcement in one form or another. Then there's Pops." He flipped over his coffee cup on the saucer to indicate to the waitress that he wanted coffee. "I don't think I've ever seen him so proud as he was the day I graduated from the academy. Out of all of us, I was the only one who followed him onto the force."

She battled against a frown. Her father had stood at the back when she graduated, then hightailed it out of there without even a congratulatory hug. She suspected he'd come only to see if she'd go through with it. "He's with M.P.D.?"

"How'd you know?"

Kelli shrugged, and crossed her fingers under the table. "Lucky guess?"

"Then you're a good guesser. Yeah, he's with the M.P.D. A thirty-five year veteran."

Thirty-five years. The same amount of time as her father. Hmm... It made her wonder if they'd met way back then.

She noticed that David hadn't said anything about his mother. Given her own experience, she was careful about asking others about family members they didn't mention on their own. She hated the awkwardness when someone asked her. Lately she'd begun saying that her mother died when she was young. It sounded better than revealing that her mother was murdered when she was seven and the killer was never caught.

Talk about a conversation stopper.

"How long you been on the force?" she asked him instead.

"Seven years. How about you?"

"Three with N.Y.P.D." She polished off the last of her dog and started on her fries.

"Do you always eat like that," he asked, motioning toward her plate.

"Like what?"

"One food group at a time? First you ate your hot dog. Then you started on your fries."

She looked down to where she held a French fry. "Yeah, I guess I do. Do you have a problem with it?"

"No. But don't you think it's a little strange?"

She pointed at his plate, which was coated with a little bit of everything he'd eaten. "Oh, and I suppose you think stuffing everything into your mouth at the same time is better."

"At least it's normal."

"Are you saying I'm not?"

He stretched his arms along the length of the booth, allowing his gaze to skim over her from head to...chest. "Oh, I'd say you're not in the least bit normal."

Kelli rolled her eyes. "Just when I begin to think you're almost human."

He sat forward and rested his forearms on the table. "You know, Kell, we still haven't talked about...well, you know, what happened the other night."

She nearly choked on her food. Deliberately taking her time, she reached for her soda, swallowed, then took a long, delaying sip. "Yes, we have. When we were partnered together."

"Oh. You're talking about when you said that we should act like it never happened."

"That's exactly what I'm talking about."

He opened his mouth to respond, but the waitress swept by and filled David's coffee cup. "Would you like any dessert today, officer?" she asked him, seeming to overlook that there were two officers at the table.

Kelli raised her brows. There was no mistaking that the waitress was offering herself up as an additional menu option. She was surprised when David didn't even take notice of the attractive blonde. Rather, he waved her away.

"Come on, Kelli, you can't be serious."

"Who says I can't?"

"I say." He sat back, causing the plastic on the booth to creak. "There isn't any departmental policy saying two officers can't...date."

She lifted a finger. "Unless those two officers are partners.

Then it's their duty to report the situation to their commanding officer and asked to be reassigned." She polished off the last of her fries and visually challenged him. "Anyway, who says I want to date?"

His eyes widened to nearly pop out of his head. "What do you mean you're not interested in dating?"

She sighed deeply, finding it difficult not to be amused by his reaction. "You know if you keep answering my question with a question, we're never going to get anywhere in this conversation."

"Well, if you start making some sense, maybe I'd stop asking so many questions."

She held up her hand. "Now I think you've just insulted me."

"This isn't about insulting anyone, Kelli."

"Don't take this personally, David, but I'm...well, I'm really not interested in dating anyone right now. So don't think it's just you. It's not. I have..." How did she put this without setting herself up for target practice? "I just got back into town. I haven't even completely unpacked yet. Now is definitely not the time to get...involved with anyone. The other night... Well, the other night was the other night. And I really do think it's a good idea if we just pretend it never happened."

She sipped on her soda, noticing the way he watched her mouth as she did so. She fought a smile, realizing she was enjoying his discomfort a tad too much.

"Come on, Kelli. Both you and I know you're not that kind of girl."

She slowly took the straw out of her mouth, satisfied by his visible swallow. "What kind of girl?"

He waved his hand. "You know what kind."

She carefully put down her cup. "You mean the kind of girl that sleeps with a guy on the first date?" She tilted her head. "Although I don't think our meeting at the bar really counts as a first date, do you? It's more like a first meeting. So what kind of girl does *that* make me?"

His grimace was so endearing she had to smile. "This isn't funny, Hatfield."

"Oh, I think it's very funny." She leaned forward this time, resting her forearms on the table between them. "Be truthful, McCoy. Would we even be having this discussion if I were a guy?"

His brows shot up high on his forehead.

She laughed. "That's not what I meant. What I'm trying to say is that you think it's perfectly all right for a guy to indulge in one-nighters, but for a woman," she shrugged, "well, it's a whole different ball game then, isn't it?"

His face relaxed, making Kelli wonder if she'd overplayed her hand. "Oh, I get it. You're trying to set me up as sexist, aren't you? You know, a primitive jerk who thinks there is one set of rules for men, quite another for women." He slowly shook his head. "Oh, no, Kell, you're not going to paint me into that losing corner." He leaned closer as well, putting them mere inches apart across the table. "Uh-uh. I'm not saying that women as a group aren't emotionally equipped for one-night stands." His gaze trailed to where she was sure her pulse was throbbing a mile a minute at her throat. "I'm saying *you* aren't."

"That's a load of crap and you know it," she said, disappointed to find her voice huskily breathless. "What you just said leads me to believe that you're a selective chauvinist. A new generation sexist. Which, in my opinion, is the worst kind." She fought the desire to tuck a wisp of hair behind her ear for fear of what the nervous gesture would reveal. "Oh, yeah, you pretend you're a new millennium man. Equal rights for women and all that. You've done your homework. Know exactly what to say and when to say it to represent yourself in this light and chuck the chauvinist argument out the window." She poked a finger against his chest. "But when all is said and done, you're as sexist as they come. A place for every woman and every woman in her place." She leaned back. As much to emphasize her point as to put some much needed distance between them. "Admit it, McCoy. You probably think a woman has no place on the force."

As in control as he appeared to be, the brief flicking away of his gaze told her she'd hit the nail right on the head. But while the lean, corded muscles in his forearms tensed, her jab barely knocked him off balance. "I'll have you know that my previous partner was a woman, Hatfield. And a damn good cop at that."

She crossed her arms over her chest, then immediately wished she hadn't as it drew his gaze there. "Uh-huh. And I'll lay ten-to-one odds that when you were due for a new partner, you thought you possibly couldn't be stuck with another woman, didn't you? That you had already done your part for equality between the sexes and that you couldn't possibly be put through that hell again."

Bull's eye. While the politically savvy David McCoy was nowhere near down for the count, she'd definitely landed a solid punch. He blinked and slowly began to sit back.

Smelling a victory, Kelli pushed her plate aside and leaned forward again. "And tell me this, David. Would we even be having this discussion if I were the one interested in repeating the other night?"

"Come again?"

She purposely ignored the double entendre of his words and cleared her throat. "I'm talking about the whole hard-to-get thing. Admit it. If I had asked for your phone number, invited you to come over last night, begged you to stay, right now you'd be running so fast in the other direction I'd have to be a marathon runner just to keep your fine butt in sight."

Uh-oh. Wrong choice of words. She knew that even before he had the chance to grin. "You think I have a fine butt?"

She scrambled to recover lost ground. "Well, that just makes two of us, doesn't it?"

"Ooooh, that was low."

She couldn't help smiling.

He slowly recrossed his arms. "So what you're telling me, Kelli Hatfield, is that the other night was no more than a one-night stand as far as you're concerned."

"Uh-huh."

"And that since we're now partners, we should just forget it ever happened."

"Yes."

"And that you're not only okay with that, you have no problem being around me without wanting to...jump my bones."

She briefly glanced away, then cringed at the dead giveaway reaction. Still, she somehow managed to hold her chin straight as she met his knowing gaze and said, "Right."

He grinned. "Wrong."

Something touched her foot under the table and she nearly jumped out of her skin, especially when she realized it was his foot.

"Oh, you're good," he said, tapping the front of her shoe with his. "But not good enough."

To her chagrin, she felt her cheeks heat. "You don't know what you're talking about."

"But you haven't even given me a chance to speak yet."

She made a production out of looking at her watch. "I think—"

"I already know what you think. Or at least what you want me to think. Now I deserve equal time, don't I?" he asked, putting the emphasis on equal.

She tried to hide her deep swallow and mentally armed herself against whatever he was about to throw at her. "Shoot."

He chuckled, the rich, wicked sound sliding down her

spine like a hot, feathery touch. Bronte was completely right when she'd said David McCoy was a pro. And she was afraid she was going to find out just how substantial his skills were.

He reached across the table and tapped the very tip of his index fingers against the sensitive skin of her hand. "I want to ask you a few questions and I ask that you be honest in your answers. No lying allowed."

She smiled enigmatically.

He groaned. "You are good at this, aren't you?"

"You sound like you think this is some sort of game."

"Well it is, isn't it? The courtship battle?"

Courtship? Kelli couldn't move her hand far away fast enough from his.

"First things first. I'd like you to tell me that what happened the other night is an ordinary, everyday occurrence for you. That your past is littered with poor guys you used as one-night stands."

Her throat tightened.

"You can't, can you? Because that night was your first night. First one-night stand, that is."

Okay, she supposed she could give him that much. "I'll admit it. It was my first one-night stand."

"Not *it. I* was your first one-night stand."

She tried to figure out where he was going with this.

He caught her pensive gaze. "Oh, no. No overanalyzing allowed. If we're going to do this, it's got to be here and now, head-to-head. No strategizing permissible."

"You can't regulate something like that."

He shrugged lightly. "You think so, huh?" At her nod, he grinned. "Okay then. You're only going to make it tougher on yourself."

She opened her mouth to ask what he meant but found out before she could get the first word out. Leaning forward with the most innocent of grace, he stretched his hands out under the table and trapped her knees in his long-fingered grasp. She gasped and tried to jerk back out of the way, but there was nowhere to go.

"Uncle," she croaked. "No strategizing."

He slowly removed his fingers.

Kelli quickly moistened her lips with a flick of her tongue. "You play dirty, McCoy."

"Whatever it takes." He shrugged. "Now, back to what I was saying. Seeing that I was your first one-night stand, then the whole modern woman argument goes right out the window. Call it a spiraling out of control, or spontaneous combustion—"

"Or a mistake in judgment," she added.

He grimaced. "Call it what you will, but don't try to play it off as if the situation was just par for the course, because I know better."

"And just how, exactly, do you know that?"

His grin widened. "I know."

Ask a dumb question, get a dumber answer.

"Anyway, I'm the one doing the asking now, remember?"

How could she forget? She looked at her watch again and he raised a brow. She sighed and sat back.

"Now that we've established that your argument is basically moot, that brings us back to the reason why you don't want to go out with me again."

"Don't you usually have to visit a subject before you can return to it?"

He leaned forward again, his hands conspicuously hidden from view.

She sat back as far as she could and murmured, "Okay, okay. No more smart comments."

"Fast learner. I like that in a woman."

She sniffed. "I'd guess there isn't a whole lot that you don't like about women."

His skillful fingers found her legs under the table, this time sliding a little higher up. She drew in a quick breath and plunged her own hands down to pluck his away. He merely trapped her hands beneath his, forcing her to lean in closer to him across the table.

His gaze flicked to where her mouth was mere inches away from his. "What was I saying? Oh, yeah. You think we shouldn't...date, for lack of a better word, because we're partners."

"Uh-huh. And don't forget that I think your continued interest in me is due solely to the fact that I'm playing hard to get."

"So you say." He hiked a brow. "*Are* you playing hard to get?"

She tried to yank her hands away from the persuasive warmth of his. "Don't be ridiculous. I'm just saying—"

"We already know what you've said." He began moving his thumb in slow circles on her lower thigh. The touch itself was maddening, but when combined with the tugging on the fabric of her slacks against certain, nearby areas...well, she was finding it increasingly difficult to concentrate. Talk about conduct unbecoming an officer. Her gaze darted around the diner, but the few people who were there weren't paying them any mind. Yet.

She needed to end this conversation and fast. "So tell me, then, David, why *do* you want to go out with me again?"

"Aside from the fact that it was the best sex I've ever had and I'd like to repeat the experience?"

"Uh-huh."

"Simply...because I like you."

He liked her. The simple words caused her heart to dip low in her belly, and intensified the growing tension between her legs. Oh, boy. She hadn't expected him to be so honest. And she had no doubt that he was. She'd expected him to pull out every weapon in his armory, but this was one she didn't know how to protect herself against.

Still, she had a few more weapons in her own arsenal. "Are you saying you want to go talk to Lieutenant Kowalsky about this?"

She felt herself regain some all-important ground with his immediate grimace. "No...I'm saying that I think we should give this thing between us a chance to see what develops."

"A couple of one-night stands," she said, growing stronger. "Uh-huh."

She moved in for the kill. Tilting her head to the side, she purposely drew the tip of her tongue along her upper lip. "What's really eating you, David? That I slept with you on the first night? Or that I slept with you and I'm not interested in seconds?"

His hands moved away from her knees so quickly, she had to laugh.

The radio on her weapons belt beeped at the same time his did, effectively slicing through the sensual web that had formed between them.

She was the first to answer. Dispatch asked if they were through with lunch and were able to take a nearby breaking and entering call.

"Got it, dispatch," she told the man.

The way David avoided her gaze, she was beginning to suspect that she'd really hurt him. Then she decided that at best she'd probably put a little ding in that monstrous ego of his, and she slid from the booth.

"We're nowhere near finished with this discussion, Hatfield," he said in a low, gravelly voice.

She blinked before looking at him, noticing the dark determination on his handsome face. Why did she have the sinking sensation that she was in way over her head with Officer David McCoy?

AT THE STATION at the end of the day, David reasoned that what happened the day before was not going to happen again. Kelli was not going to duck out on him. Not when they had their...discussion to finish.

Even though four and a half hours and five official calls separated now from their time at the diner, he still felt vaguely like he should be doubled over from the beating he'd taken during that conversation.

Pretending an interest in talking to a fellow male officer, he covertly watched Kelli hang her weapons belt in her locker in the next row. She was closer to the door, but he was coming to accept that he was at a permanent disadvantage where Kelli Hatfield was concerned. He'd just have to compensate for it.

She looked in his direction and he offered up a quick grin. Her slightly smug return smile put him on alert. She'd been giving him that smile all afternoon. At one point he'd been sorely tempted to pull the patrol car to the side of the road and kiss the damnable expression from her delectable little face.

Oh no, Kelli definitely didn't fit into the "sugar and spice and everything nice" category, as he had made the mistake of believing the other night. No, vinegar, jalapenos and red pepper were part of what went into making her. And, damn it all, the recipe made him even hungrier for her.

She closed her locker and made a beeline for the door. David slammed his own locker door shut and hurried after her.

"Hatfield, hold up!" he called out.

She quickened her step.

But no matter what mental ground he may have lost, physically he was still way ahead of the game. She didn't dare break into a run within the station house without raising suspicion, and his long strides quickly brought him next to her.

"Where are you going?"

Her grimace was altogether appealing. "Home. Alone."

That's what *she* thought. If he had it his way, he'd be tag-

ging there right along with her. But he was going to have to
do some quick stepping before that had a remote possibility
of happening.

He plowed right into a fellow officer. Speaking of stepping, he'd better concentrate on where he was going right
now.

Mumbling an apology, he began to skirt around the ob-
struction when he realized that the wall blocking his way
was none other than Lieutenant Kowalsky.

"Officers Hatfield and McCoy. Just the two people I was
looking for." He looked up to find Kow grinning. "You mind
removing yourself from my uniform, boy?"

Damn. David's gaze slid from the towering man to his
new partner. Remembering their words at the diner, he wondered if she'd gone ahead and said something to their superior officer anyway. Not because she was interested in pur-
suing a further relationship with him, but because she was
the type who would be on the up-and-up in any situation.
And she probably viewed the circumstances surrounding
their odd relationship as compromising.

Double damn.

His suspicions only deepened when Kow focused his gaze
on Kelli. "First of all, I want to congratulate you, Officer Hatfield. Second official day on the job and you've already been
promoted—temporarily, of course."

"Sir?" both David and Kelli said simultaneously.

"The special task force, Hatfield. You nabbed yourself a
spot. You're to report in for briefing bright and early, as they
say."

"You put in for the task force?" David asked, incredulous.

Kelli beamed at him, her smile a little too wide, her eyes a
little too full of mischief. "What did you think I was doing
when I kept you waiting this morning? Powdering my
nose?"

Geez...

"You can't," he said vehemently, surprising even himself.

Her eyes instantly narrowed and the hall went, suddenly, deafeningly silent. "Define 'can't,' Officer McCoy," she said finally.

He shrugged ineffectually, searching for a reason that would make some sort of sense. Only problem was, he couldn't put it into words. He only knew what he felt, and that was until he knew her a little better, trusted what she was capable of, he didn't want to see her put in any unnecessary danger. And that damn task force assignment had danger written all over it. "I don't know. You just can't accept that spot on the task force. I won't allow it."

"Pardon me, but just when, exactly, were you put in charge of my decisions?"

"Since I became your partner."

She appeared on the verge of laughter. "That's rich, coming from a guy who doesn't even know what the meaning of the word is."

"She's got you there, officer." Kow seemed to find their exchange as amusing as Kelli now apparently did. "I didn't see your name on the list of potential candidates, McCoy. Why is that?"

"Because I like my uniform just fine, thank you." And he thought Kelli did, too. What was all her talk about equality between the sexes if the first thing she did was run off and join up with the task force?

Kowalsky's chuckle got under his skin. "And your uniform likes you, too, McCoy—most of the time." He pulled a pack of gum out of his front shirt pocket, then offered them a piece. They both shook their heads. "Since Officer Hatfield here will no longer be available to be your partner, I've taken the liberty of matching you up with someone else. Phillips has opted for a desk job until after she comes back from maternity leave, so that leaves Johnson minus one partner. I think you two are a match made in heaven. If everything goes the way I expect, and there's no reason for me to believe otherwise, then you'll both get your partners back at the same time."

"Johnson?" David repeated.

"Yep. First thing in the morning." He popped a piece of gum into his mouth and chewed with immense satisfaction. "Got a problem with that, officer?"

David scratched his head. "No. No, sir, I guess I don't."

"Good."

Kelli thrust her hand forward and enthusiastically pumped Kow's. "Thank you, sir, for allowing me to accept the position with the task force. You won't be sorry."

"I know I won't, Hatfield. I just hope the same applies to you."

The big man neatly continued on his way down the hall.

David could do little more than stand cemented to the spot as Kelli waggled her fingers at him and went the other way.

5

ANOTHER NOTE. Kelli plucked it from where it was stuck in the
jamb of her door and slid it inside one of her shopping bags. A
full day had passed since she'd left David standing in the station hall looking like a bomb victim. She didn't have to read the
note to know what it said. "We need to talk," signed D., were
the words on the last two notes, one left last night, another this
morning. It was likely what this one said, too.

"What was that?" Bronte asked, trying to sneak a peek over
Kelli's shoulder.

Kelli jiggled the bag so the note fell down to the bottom. Just
because the guy monopolized her thoughts every minute of
every day didn't mean she was up to sharing that piece of information with her best friend. "Nothing. Only the landlord
telling me when the rent's due."

She led the way through the open door, leaving Bronte to
close it behind her. "Uh-huh. You just moved in and the landlord's worried about the rent. Sure, I'll buy that one." She ges-
tured to the bags. "I figure I should buy something, considering all the money you just spent."

"I didn't know how much fun it would be to spend the department's money." Kelli dropped her shopping bags on the
couch, then collapsed alongside them. "Have I ever told you
that you have a suspicious mind?" she said, slipping off her
coat.

Bronte hung it along with her own sleek pale leather jacket
on the tree next to the door, then she dropped into the chair

across from Kelli. "Comes with the territory." She cast a glance around the apartment. "Are you ever planning to unpack?"

Grimacing, Kelli took in the boxes stacked in every available spot in the place. There were three clear paths. One that ran from the doorway to the couch and on into the kitchen. Another to the bathroom. The third to her bedroom. "Are you volunteering to help?"

Bronte laughed. "Not in this lifetime. I have enough trouble keeping up with my own place." She rolled her head to look at her, her short red hair immediately falling back into place.

Kojak came panting down the path from the kitchen and plopped his plump butt at Kelli's feet. She heartily rubbed the dog's jowls and made kiss-kiss noises at him.

Bronte made a face. "Have I ever told you how disgusting that is? I don't get that close to the men I date." She leaned forward and emptied out the contents of one of the bags onto the floor. "So I take it you're not going to tell me who the note was really from then."

Kelli smiled. "Nope."

She wrinkled her nose. "Heartless witch." She picked up a miniskirt and turned it first one way, then another. "Just remember that when you're curious about what's going on with my life and I tell you to buzz off. Are you really going to wear this?"

Kelli snatched the skirt from her fingers. "I don't have to remember it because I already know there's absolutely nothing going on in your life. Hasn't been for at least six months. And yes, I'm going to wear that. It's part of my job." She grimaced at the scrap of red suede. Knowing it was right for her temporary reassignment was one thing, actually shimmying into the thing was quite another. She tossed it onto the couch. Too late for second thoughts. "By the way, why isn't anything going on with your life?"

"Ha!" Bronte flipped the strap of a jewel blue Wonderbra

around and around her index finger. "The author of the note first."

"God, did I really buy that?"

Bronte positioned it like a sling shot and launched it at her. It landed on Kojak's head. "Yep. I was there so there's no denying it."

Kelli collected the bra before the dog could catch the silky fabric in his slobbery jaws. He got up, ran this way, then that, down the only path available to him, then barked. "No, you can't have it. Sheesh, buy the pooch a million play toys and he salivates after my bra."

Bronte hiked a feathery red brow. "That's a male for you."

Kojak lengthened his pacing to reach the door and barked again.

"You know—"

"Shh," Kelli said, holding out her hand. "Be quiet a sec." Kojak stopped at the door and began scratching at the bottom of it. The evidence of claw marks on the bottom of the wood told Kelli it wasn't the first time. She rolled her eyes.

"What is it?" Bronte said in a stage whisper.

Kelli waved her away. "I think someone's outside."

Her friend's blue eyes twinkled. "The landlord?"

She threw an embroidered pillow at Bronte. The landlord, indeed. Bronte knew exactly who had written the note without her having said anything. Not that it would take a genius to figure it out. She'd been back in town a whole five days, and two of those she'd spent moving in. The other three had included a maddeningly sexy, egotistical, insufferable man named David McCoy. Sometimes it stunk having a friend who knew everything about you.

Kojak barked, making Kelli jump. Then his stumpy tail started wagging like crazy. She watched as something small and round rolled under the door—something the dog happily gobbled up.

"I can't believe it!" she whispered. "You little traitor." She had trouble enough getting him to eat his special diet food now. With a certain conniving someone feeding him treats under the door, he'd be impossible to live with.

A quick, clear knock, then, "Kelli?" filtered through the door. "I know you're in there, so you might as well just open up."

Ignoring the two males that occupied more of her time than she liked, Kelli started unpacking the bags on the couch next to her. Black leather-like pants. Low-cut vests. Clingy tops in various rich gemstone shades began piling up next to her. "You know, I'm still not really sure about this one," she said, holding up a dress for Bronte to see. "Do you think it suits me?"

"I think it makes you look like a ten-dollar whore." She smiled. "It's perfect."

"Yeah, well, the only reason I bought it was because you insisted."

"And now I'm insisting you keep it." Bronte stood up and molded the decadent scrap of material against herself. "If only so I can borrow it." She draped the dress alongside the rest of the clothes.

Another brief rap on the door. "Just so you know, Kell, I'm going to stay out here until you talk to me."

Kelli avoided Bronte's curious gaze. She picked up a pair of black platform shoes, then slid her feet out of her practical loafers. "God, I don't even know if I can walk in these, much less run."

"Kel-li," David dragged her name out.

Bronte laughed. "Are you going to let the sad sack of lust in, or leave him hanging out there all day?"

"Leave him hanging?"

"Oooo, who'd have thought you'd be so shamelessly... wicked?"

"Oh, shut up, Bronte." She glanced at her watch. "Give him twenty minutes. He'll go away. He always does."

Bronte flopped back down in the chair. "Always? For God's sake, Kell, how long has this been going on?"

She shrugged. "Since last night." More specifically, three times last night, then two times this morning before she'd even gotten up. She hadn't been pleased when he'd awoken her from the first good sleep she'd had since the night they'd spent together. Especially since that sleep had included decadent images of them doing everything but sleeping. His mouth planted on hers. His toned, hot body stretched out alongside hers. The evidence of his desire for her pressed against the soft, sensitive skin of her belly. Images she could at least enjoy while sleeping, but fantasies she didn't dare indulge in in the real world.

"Uh-huh." Bronte thoughtfully stroked the material of a silky teddy, then dangled the wicked slip of material from her index finger. "This for work? Or for more...depraved purposes?"

Kelli snatched the most self-indulgent of her purchases from her friend's hand. "If you're asking if I'm going to charge the department for it...no."

"That's not what I'm asking and you know it."

"I'm tired of sleeping in old, torn T-shirts. Is that all right with you?"

They both heard the shuffle of feet outside the door. "What? What did you buy?"

Both women looked at each other then burst out laughing.

"Just so long as you're in bed...alone, I don't see a problem with the purchase. I have a dresser full just like it." Bronte frowned. "Though I've come to prefer the old, tattered T-shirts, myself."

"See, that's just what I mean. You're no fun anymore," Kelli told her. "Speaking of which. Since you now know the identity of my...secret admirer," she heard a sharp curse from the other side of the door, "that means you have to answer my question. Why the dull love life lately?

"I'd have to have a love life for it to qualify as dull," Bronte corrected. "No, I'd say my love life is pretty much nonexistent right now."

"Which is a nonanswer. Come on, Bron. What gives? In the entire history of our friendship, I don't think I've ever seen you go without a man for more than a few days at a stretch. What gives?"

She shrugged, but there was nothing remotely nonchalant about the gesture. "I don't know. Maybe I thought it was time I finally started to see myself outside the confining bonds of a relationship. Get to know who I was, rather than who I was pretending to be for a man's sake."

She shook her head. "Uh-uh. Too philosophical for you. Come on, Bron, you've always known who you are. You may have come to the conclusions you've just cited since you stopped dating, but what I want to know is the main catalyst. Something had to have happened."

"Maybe."

Kelli gazed thoughtfully at her friend. Even when she lived in New York they'd remained close. Phone calls nearly every other day. Spontaneous visits. Despite the distance that separated them, they'd always maintained a closeness she treasured. Well, except when it came to men like David McCoy.

She tried to remember what was going on six months ago. The only thing she could recall was that Bronte had been steadily dating a mystery man she refused to share much about. Kelli remembered being somewhat surprised by the lack of information from her usually very talkative friend, but she hadn't thought much of it. She'd thought Bronte would share when she was ready, though she never had gotten to that point. Instead, one day she lightly said that they'd broken up and that she'd moved on to greener pastures.

Kelli wondered if they were greener, lonelier pastures.

"It's that guy, isn't it? That one you wouldn't talk about?"

Bronte's cheeks reddened and she knew that she was right.

"You're wrong. This isn't just about some guy, Kelly. This is about me."

"What guy?"

The question came from the hallway, letting them know they weren't exactly alone.

Bronte rolled her eyes and laughed. "You know, you probably should talk to him. Let him get whatever he has to say off his chest so you can get on with your life without some moron sitting on your doorstep."

"I heard that," came David's muffled response.

Kelli smiled. "I already know what he has on his chest...and elsewhere," she said teasingly. She leaned forward, lowering her voice for Bronte's ears only, though she said little more than this girl talk was probably driving him bonkers.

"Really?" Bronte asked, playing along.

Something clunked against the door, then David groaned. "What? What did she say?"

Kelli's smile widened as she began stacking her new undercover wardrobe back into one bag.

Bronte cleared her throat, then asked softly, "What's really going on, Kelli?"

"Simple. He didn't think I was a capable cop, now he thinks I'm insane for accepting this position on the task force."

"That makes two of us."

"The difference being I'm still letting you into the apartment."

Bronte raised a finger. "Important detail, that one."

Kelli started to get up. "Want some coffee?"

"I do," David said from the other side of the door.

"Tough," Kelli said, then cringed when she realized she'd spoken to him directly. And here she had been doing so well ignoring him. She stalked to the door, but rather than opening it, she curled her fingers around Kojak's collar and dragged him unwillingly toward the kitchen where she planned to close up the little traitor.

A short while later, after Bronte told Kelli about her latest case with the U.S. attorney's office and Kelli gave her some advice on effective personal protection devices, they noticed their conversation had dwindled down to the two of them.

Bronte glanced at her watch. "Took longer than twenty minutes, I think."

Kelli grimaced. "I think that's because he had an audience."

"Speaking of audiences, I have to go put in an appearance at the Senior U.S. Attorney's Christmas party tonight. And if I hope to look drop-dead gorgeous—a three-hour job at least—I'd better get running."

"You always look great."

Bronte looked her over. "Yeah, but my kind of beauty takes work. Yours...you have this girl-next-door look going on that not even a week at the Estee Lauder counter can give me."

Kelli got up with her. "I better go make sure the coast is clear first. Lord knows what'll happen if a certain somebody gets a hold of you outside the door."

"You're worried about me?"

Kelli draped an arm over her shoulders. "I'm worried about him."

They laughed as Bronte shrugged into her coat. Kelli made a production out of looking through the peephole. She firmly told herself she wasn't disappointed when she found the hall and surrounding stairs empty. She quietly unlocked the door and opened it. A quick peek found no sexy David lurking in the shadows.

Damn.

"Okay," she said, turning to Bronte. "All clear." She gave her friend a quick hug. She was about to pull away when she changed her mind and gave her a heartier one. She stood like that for long moments, just squeezing.

Bronte slowly drew away. "What was that for?"

Kelli smiled. "I don't know. You looked like maybe you needed it."

Judging by the moisture in her dear, dear friend's eyes, she suspected she'd guessed right.

Kelli straightened the lapels of Bronte's coat. "Call me, later, huh? No matter what time you get in. You know, so you can give me the full scoop on whose wife was wearing what, which husband was caught banging his secretary in the broom closet, and which idiot fell into the punch bowl."

Was it her, or was Bronte's laugh a little shaky? "Okay."

Kelli watched her walk down the steps, then she closed the door and leaned against it. She knew there was much more involved in Bronte's decision to stay seriously single, but she hadn't a clue how to go about getting her to share the information. Her friend had never kept anything from her before. The fact that she was now alerted Kelli to the seriousness of the situation. But until she knew what had happened there was very little she could do beyond letting Bronte know that she was there for her. And she intended to do that at least twice a day now that she was back in town and long distance carriers weren't involved.

The sound of scratching came from behind the kitchen door. Kelli sighed and figured she'd better let Kojak loose before she ended up either staying in the apartment for the rest of her life, or replacing all the doors when she eventually moved out.

She propped open the swinging door and stared down at the little criminal. "You're in big trouble, mister."

Kojak comically backed up, then plopped his full-size behind on the floor, his pitiful whine combined with a bored yawn. She laughed, then bent over and gave him a playful tousle. She waggled a finger in front of his watery eyes. "No more treats for you. One year," she said.

He barked, then played nip-the-ankle while she washed the coffee cups. Afterward she went back into the living room to attack a few of the easier boxes. And seeing as Christmas was less than a week away, she should probably think about decorating a bit. She considered the far corner. A small tree would be nice.

But first she felt an inexplicable need to get her life back into some sort of order and that meant unpacking essentials. Like her neon purple sports water bottle.

The only problem was that an hour and six boxes later she felt no more at peace than she did before she started, water bottle notwithstanding. Plunging her hands deep into box seven, with Kojak attacking pieces of crumpled old packing newspaper like they were small, predatory animals, she wondered just how she had accumulated so much stuff, and how she could go about getting rid of it all.

She drew her finger along an antique frame that held an old, professional shot of her and her parents taken when she was five.

A knock at the door startled her.

Kojak looked up and made a Scooby-Doo-style sound of inquiry, then ran, barking, to the door.

"Oh, no, you don't," Kelli said, hurrying after him.

After several unsuccessful attempts to stop him from scratching at the bottom of the door to get at his new friend, Kelli snapped upright, sighed, then yanked the door open wide.

"I've had just about as much of this as I'm going to take, Mc-Coy. Get this through your thick, stubborn head right now. I am not going to sl—"

The word died halfway out of her mouth, leaving her feeling like she'd just choked on something very bitter indeed. Because rather than staring into the too-handsome features of one yummy David McCoy, she instead gaped at the very familiar face of her father. He was definitely as startled as she was. And he was dressed to the nines in his complete police uniform.

WHOA. THAT COULDN'T be who he thought it was…could it?

David crouched down lower in the front seat of his old

Mustang, eyeing the familiar figure leaving Kelli's apartment building. There was no mistaking Assistant Chief Garth Hatfield, or ignoring the glowering expression he wore as he looked both ways down the street. David slid down a little lower and cringed. The action made him feel like he'd just been caught sneaking a peek under Little Miss Muffet's tuffet.

Hatfield walked to a four-door sedan, then got in, his movements quick and precise. Within moments he was driving away.

David expelled a long breath. Boy, if he thought yesterday was a bad day, today was turning out even worse. He'd sunk to a new low hanging around outside Kelli's apartment, but he didn't see that he had any choice. He'd reasoned that things had to improve for him sooner or later, right?

Wrong.

He brought his forehead down on the steering wheel with a clunk, ignoring the spicy Mexican food that sat in a large bag on the passenger seat. Given all the trouble he was having with someone by the name of Hatfield, he should have quickly connected the dots and brought her together with one Garth Hatfield, Regional Assistant Chief for the East. But ever since meeting Kelli that night at the bar, his entire equilibrium seemed to be off-kilter. Hell, who was he kidding? He was having a hard enough time keeping upright with all that was going on.

Despite all that, he wasn't about to delude himself into thinking Garth Hatfield had been visiting someone else in the apartment building.

He didn't know what he'd done in this lifetime or any other to deserve this abuse, but whatever it was, it must have been a doozy.

"Pops is going to have a fit," he muttered.

Pulling back from the steering wheel, he stared through the now fogged windshield at the empty street blanketed with a moderate covering of snow. Oh, he knew of the feud between Sean McCoy and Garth Hatfield. It was impossible to be anywhere on the M.P.D. and not know of it. Not that he'd ever discovered what the feud was about. Pops had got so worked up when he'd brought it up over dinner one night, David was afraid he might choke on his mashed potatoes. But in the years since, he'd unearthed a few small, insignificant details. Such as the two men had been best friends when they went through the academy together. They were from the same neighborhood in north D.C., having grown up no more than two blocks apart. And that if time and circumstances ever found them in the same room together now, they'd likely do each other bodily harm.

The revelation had amused him in the beginning. Pops was so levelheaded about everything else that this little feud had been his own personal ace in the hole. The card he used whenever he wanted to change the subject.

Thankfully he'd only had one run-in with Sean's adversary. And it hadn't been pretty. It was his first year on the force and after the successful collaring of three armed robbery suspects he'd been barreling into the station at the same time Hatfield had been coming out. Damned if he didn't plow straight into the old man. He hadn't yet learned to distinguish between the stars and bars on a uniform. Not that it mattered, because Hatfield hadn't been wearing his full "u." He'd been in plain shirtsleeves and dark slacks and looked about as cocky as David had felt at that particular moment. David had none too politely suggested he watch where he was going. It was then his partner at the time had pointed out the error of his ways and respectfully acknowledged the chief. Hatfield had asked them to introduce themselves. And when he'd heard the name McCoy, he looked...well, pretty much how Pops had looked that night when he'd first mentioned Hatfield's name.

No, it definitely hadn't been pretty.

Someone rapped on the window. David jumped, half expecting Garth Hatfield to be standing outside, palming the revolver in his weapons belt. Instead he found a beat cop pointing at the no parking sign he sat in front of. David flipped out his own ID and plastered it against the window. The officer smiled and gave him a thumbs-up.

David watched him walk on down the street. A part of the normal routine? Or did Daddy have extra protection on his baby's block?

When another squad car slowly drove by, giving him a long look, David decided firmly on the latter.

Not only was he involved, or very desperately wanted to be involved, with his own partner, that same partner was the daughter of a D.C. Metropolitan Police chief.

Could things get any worse?

He figured they couldn't.

He stared at the brightly lit third-floor window. But that didn't mean they couldn't get any better.

Grinning, he grabbed the bag of Mexican food and opened the car door.

6

KELLI SAT ON the arm of the couch staring at the opposite wall. Only a short while before she'd hung her academy certificate there, and positioned black-and-white professionally framed photos of D.C. around it. Not that she saw any of them. She could concentrate on little more than the visit she'd just suffered through with her father.

Ever since she was twenty and made her intention to join the force known, a tension had stretched between her and Garth Hatfield that strained like the steel cables holding together a suspension bridge. Over the years she'd come not only to accept the tension, she'd learned how to carefully balance her need to be a police officer with her father's need to protect his only child. Had even come to enjoy their little tugs-of-war, their endless debates over their differences of opinion, and had taken comfort in knowing that despite everything, he'd always be there for her.

But tonight...

Wow.

She'd known the instant she'd opened the door that she'd made a big time error. But she'd been completely unprepared for her father's nuclear meltdown at the knowledge that one certain David McCoy, of the hated McCoys, not only knew where she lived but was an expected visitor. She'd been unable to do anything more than blink at him as his handsome face had turned an unhealthy shade of red while he'd stood in her hallway and lit into her.

"You better get this straight, missy. I may have to put up

with your being a police officer. And now your stupid notion of getting involved in that godforsaken task force, but this... Are you seeing that uncivilized slug?"

"Slug?" she'd practically coughed, slightly amused at that point, though still stinging at her blunder.

"You heard me, girl."

His penchant for calling her "girl" had really never bothered her. Up until that point he'd used it as an endearment like honey or darling. But this time it came out sounding condescending and derogatory, and something within her bristled. She'd stubbornly crossed her arms and said, "Well, excuse me if I don't answer your question, Daddy, but I don't see that my personal life is any of your business."

Now Kelli cringed as she rubbed her forehead. She supposed she really shouldn't have baited him that way, not knowing how upset he already was. But who knew he would blow a gasket over her perfectly vague statement?

Kojak whined, then stuck his head out from where he'd been cowering in her bedroom. His tongue lolled out of his mouth as he checked to see if the coast was clear.

"A cease-fire has been declared," she told him, then silently added, "for now."

The dog happily made his way across the wood floor, his nails clicking, then plopped down near the door.

Kelli considered him. "Do you want to go for a walk, K?"

If she didn't know better, she'd think he'd shaken his head. No. It was probably his version of a canine sneeze. He looked at the door then whined again.

Kelli's gaze zoomed in on the thick white wood. *Don't tell me...*

Pushing from the sofa arm, she followed Kojak's lead. Frowning, she reached over him, much to his tail-wagging delight, and pulled open the door.

Just as she suspected. David stood on the other side, hand

raised to knock, his eyes as large as his badge. What she didn't expect was the rush of warmth and pleasure at seeing him.

"I didn't even knock yet," he said.

Kelli motioned toward his new buddy.

"Oh." He reached down and patted the dog, then straightened and held up a white bag. "Hungry?"

She curved her arms around her upper torso. "Not particularly." She turned and walked back into the apartment. "But you might as well come in. You can't possibly be any worse than my last visitor." She partially turned and jabbed a finger in his direction. "But no funny stuff, you hear?"

"Got it."

She heard the door close behind him and continued on into the kitchen, emerging seconds later with two bottles of beer. She handed him one, then took a long, needy pull from the other.

"That bad, huh?" he asked.

She sat back down on the sofa arm, gazing at where he was sprawled all too attractively in the chair across from her. "If you only knew."

He raised his bottle in a silent toast to her, then took a sip. "Actually, I think I do."

She eyed him. She wasn't exactly sure why she'd let him in. Perhaps in childish rebellion against her father. Maybe because she felt somewhat guilty about making him sit outside her apartment all afternoon. Whatever the reason, she'd be well served to remember he was still her sexual enemy.

But she couldn't ignore the part of her that wanted him to be her friend. "How so?" she asked.

He grimaced as he put his bottle down on the coffee table. "I don't know if I should admit it because I'm feeling a little stupid that I didn't put two and two together before now."

Kelli closed her eyes and groaned. "You saw my father, didn't you?"

He sighed and grabbed the bag. "Yeah."

Oh, no. "You didn't run into him or anything, did you?" She searched his face, looking for physical evidence that Garth Hatfield had done as he promised he would do, which was show that lover boy McCoy that he shouldn't be messing where he didn't belong. As angry as he was, she was half afraid he would pull David's address from department personnel records and head over there for a one-on-one battle tonight.

He started routing around in the paper bags. "No. I just saw him leaving. Don't worry, he didn't see me, so there's no reason to think he knows anything about us."

Kelli looked down, her cheeks flaming.

The rustle of paper stopped. Kelli looked to find him staring at her, his hands stopped midmotion. "I think this is where you're supposed to say that there is no us."

Her spine snapped straight. "There is no us."

A wrapped something or other in hand, he flopped back against the cushions, oblivious to the fact that Kojak had stuck his head into the bag. "Oh, hell, Kell, don't tell me that you told him."

"Told him what?" She snatched the bag away from Kojak. "There's nothing to tell." She rummaged around inside, finding Mexican food. She nearly groaned out loud. It had been eons since she'd had good Mexican, and this definitely smelled good. "This for me?"

"Knock yourself out." David waved a distracted hand. "So what did you tell him?"

She shrugged. "Well, I didn't exactly tell him anything. I just kind of alluded to the fact that there might be something between us, that's all."

"Alluded?"

She glared at him. "I had to do something after I virtually called him your name when I answered the door."

She watched a grin edge across his exceptionally handsome

face. "You didn't? Oh, what I would have given to be there when you did that."

She unwrapped a burrito dripping with cheese and snorted. "Be glad you weren't or else you wouldn't have any teeth left to chew with."

The grin vanished.

Kelli concentrated on her food and David did the same, silence falling between them. She rolled her eyes when he fed a taco, lettuce and all, to Kojak. At this rate the dog was going to follow him home. And then where would she be?

What a sorry life she led.

She'd moved on to a delectable fajita and pointed it at him. "You know, you could have said something about this stupid...rivalry thing going on between my dad and yours."

"You forget, I didn't know your dad was your dad until just now," he said. "And it's a feud."

"Cute. Anyway, I didn't find out anything until the other day when Dad found out you were my partner."

"I bet he was happy."

"Yeah," she took a long sip of beer, then stared at the bottle. "He mentioned something about busting one of these over your dad's head."

"You're kidding."

"Nope."

He leaned his forearms against his jean-clad knees. "He didn't happen to share what started this feud, did he?"

Her gaze flicked to his. "You mean you don't know?"

"Uh-uh. I just know that the feelings your father has for mine are returned two hundred fold—which is weird, because Pops gets along with everyone."

"So does my dad."

David hiked a dark blond brow.

"Well, most people anyway," she qualified. "At any rate, I've never heard him voice the sort of antagonism he feels for your dad before."

They continued eating in silence. It wasn't until every last morsel was gone, and Kelli had gone to fetch fresh beer, that she said, "You know, after this I might even believe you're half human."

He grinned and accepted the beer. "What do you mean?"

She sank down onto the couch across from him and rested her bare feet against the edge of the coffee table. "You've been here for what? A half an hour at least and there's a bed," she pointed the neck of her bottle toward her bedroom door, "not twenty feet away and you haven't once tried to get me into it."

"Yet," he added.

She couldn't help her smile or the sizzling, hopeful heat that warmed her upper thighs.

"Hey, even a guy like me knows some things about women."

"You know jack."

"Your words a minute ago say differently."

She shook her head. "No, I said you might be half human. I didn't breathe one word about your sexual prowess, or lack thereof."

He groaned. "You don't know what it does to me just hearing you say the word 'sexual.'"

As she looked over at him, Kelli couldn't ignore the slow burn in her belly that had nothing to do with the spicy food she'd just devoured. The guy was better looking than any one man had a right to be. She forced her gaze away and found herself staring at the notes resting on the side of the table. "Okay, McCoy, now that you have my undivided attention, talk."

"Talk?"

She stared at the ceiling. "Isn't that the reason you've spent half the afternoon parked out in my hall? Why you've left four notes at least—"

"Three."

"Three then. Why you've left three notes on my door saying we needed to do exactly that."

"Talk?"

She nodded and smiled around her beer bottle as she took another sip. The magic golden liquid was beginning to spiral its way through her bloodstream, relaxing her, making her bolder than she should be.

He lifted himself from his semisprawled position, placed his bottle down on the table, then looked her squarely in the face. "Okay, then. I think you need to forget about this task force stuff and come back to being my partner."

Kelli nearly spewed the contents of her mouth across his serious face.

DAVID WATCHED Kelli's expression go from shock, to amusement, then melt into what it was now, somewhere between anger and disgust.

"You've got to be kidding," she said, taking her tiny, sexy feet from the table and mimicking his posture.

He shook his head. "I'm serious as a heart attack, baby."

She sprang from the couch so quickly he moved back. Strictly as a defensive maneuver, even though five feet and a coffee table separated them. She stalked over to the dining room table behind him, forcing him to turn in order to keep her in view. And, oh, what a view it was, too. Despite the topic of their conversation, he'd spent the past half hour wrestling with his libido and basically stopping himself from lunging across the way and plastering his mouth against her luscious one.

She opened a manila folder but he doubted she saw the contents. His gaze slid to her nicely rounded bottom under the loose fit of her jeans. He could just make out the high cut of her panties under the soft fabric.

He turned back to face forward, taking the quiet moment to look around the place. Since he was last there she'd somehow managed to make the place look like a home. There were still a couple of boxes stacked up in the corner of the dining area, but overall he suspected she was almost done. At his feet was a colorful area rug stretching from his chair to the sofa. On the walls were pictures and photographs artfully hung so as to compliment the decor of the apartment rather than detract from it. And through the bedroom door he saw that she'd finally made the bed they'd spent so much time in the other night. A blue and white striped comforter, a white bed skirt, and a few accent rugs made the room look all too inviting.

Kelli had made the comment that not once had he tried to get her in there in the past half hour. Well, he didn't know what she'd think if he told her it had taken Herculean effort not to toss her over his shoulder and carry her off into that room. Oh sure, he suspected she initially would have fought him like a she-cat. But he had little doubt that all that restless energy would then have been channeled into some pretty sublime sex.

He ran his hand over his face. They might have been in that room right now if he hadn't gone and opened his stupid mouth. But he suspected if he tried anything now, she'd just as soon shoot him.

Speaking of which...

He gave the apartment another cursory glance but nowhere did he see evidence that she kept a revolver tucked away anywhere. Then again, what had he expected? For her to have a slew of them displayed on the wall? His own weapons belt was at his apartment hanging on the coat tree just inside the door.

He cleared his throat, growing more uncomfortable with her silent treatment. "Well, aren't you going to say anything?" he asked.

She slowly closed the file, then turned to face him. "When you say something worthy of a response, I will."

He rested his head against the back of the tan chair. "Come on, Kell, you have to know I'm saying this for your own good. You're out of your element as a uniform. But at least when you're there I can keep an eye out for you."

Uh-oh. Wrong thing to say. He could see it on her face.

She stalked back to stand directly in front of him. "You seem to forget that I got along just fine in New York for three years without you, McCoy."

"That's different."

"Oh? How so?"

"I wasn't there."

She threw her hands up in a way that made her breasts bounce under the soft wool of her green sweater. "You are just too much, you know that, McCoy?" She caught him looking at her chest and firmly crossed her arms to cover it. "Forget it."

He looked at her. "Forget what?"

"I'm not going to quit the task force."

He grimaced. "Just what do you have to prove, Hatfield?"

"I don't have to prove anything. But I am hoping to achieve something. If this works out the way I'm hoping it will, I'll have a detective's shield faster than I planned."

Detective's shield? Is that what all this was about? He opened his mouth to say the words, but she rushed on.

"So you can just take your request and stick it where the sun don't shine, McCoy, do you hear me? I don't need any macho man, station-house-hotshot lady-killer thinking he needs to look after me like I'm some simpering wimp unable to protect myself. I'll have you know I've seen my share of scrapes and hairy moments."

"Yeah?" He eyed her slender body.

"Yeah."

He couldn't help his grin. "Prove it."

She lifted her sweater to hover just below her rib cage, revealing a puckered scar. "See that? A twenty-two at close range."

"Hmm." He leaned in to get a closer look. The tiny flaw on her otherwise silky skin turned him on beyond belief.

She quickly turned around. "And this?" she said, tugging on the waist of her jeans to reveal a cute little dimple. He tore his gaze away from it and to where she pointed to a thin red line. "I took a serrated knife to the back."

"Hmm," he said again, running his fingertip along the length of it.

He felt her involuntary shiver and grinned.

Before she could object, he grasped her hips, swiveled her around, then tugged until she was sprawled across his lap. "All those scars prove, Hatfield, is that you need me to look after your cute little behind all the more." He slid a hand up the back of her leg to cup the area in question.

She gasped.

God but she flushed the most attractive shade of red when she was angry.

He braced himself for her counterattack. There were any number of defensive maneuvers she could use to free herself from his grasp. The one he hadn't counted on was her pressing her mouth hungrily against his.

David groaned and slid his hand up to cup the back of her head. It was empowering to know that while he'd been biding his time, waiting for the exact right moment to make his move, all along Kelli had wanted him as badly as he wanted her.

He thrust his tongue into her mouth with a bold, thorough stroke. It was impossible that she tasted even better than he remembered, but she did. So good, in fact, that he wondered how he had survived this long without devouring her. Her fingers pushed up the fabric of his shirt and he caught his breath, cracking his eyelids to find her watching him, her green, green eyes holding all the hunger he felt.

She hauled her mouth from his, her lips damp, her breathing ragged. "This is crazy, you know?"

He smiled and pressed his lips against the very corner of one side of her mouth, then the other. "I know."

And he kissed her again, thinking the word crazy about summed everything up. He was crazy with lust for her. Crazy with need. Crazy about her, period. Everything about her. Her prickly defensiveness. Her unpredictable passion. Her ability to cut him down to size with no more than a few words...or with a simple kiss from her delicious mouth.

Something brushed against his leg. David nearly jumped clear out of his skin as he hauled his mouth from Kelli's and stared down at where Kojak avidly watched them, his panting tongue curving up against his nose.

David threw back his head and laughed.

Kelli got up. It was all he could do not to yank her back down. "Oh, no, Jackie boy, this is not something your innocent eyes should be seeing."

David's heated gaze followed Kelli as she shut the dog into the kitchen, her words sending his pulse rate soaring off the charts. She turned, stopped, then pulled her sweater over her head, tousling her blond hair and revealing a purple satin bra that enhanced rather than concealed her breasts. She tossed the sweater to the dining room table then continued walking toward him. He nearly died when she dropped to her knees between his legs and began tugging at his leather belt. But he was nowhere near patient enough for whatever she may have had in mind. As soon as she held his throbbing shaft in her soft little palm, he hauled her back up onto his lap and with impatient tugs and pulls freed her of her own jeans, his mouth seeking the breasts swaying in front of his hungry eyes.

Then finally he was safely sheathed and was filling her. Her heat surrounded him. Her sleek muscles expanding and contracting as she adjusted to his size.

He grasped her hips, holding her there, holding her still as he gritted his teeth. "Hold up, Kell. Let a man catch his breath."

Her sexy little smile nearly toppled him right over the edge. "Oh no, McCoy. You're not the one calling the shots this time." She rocked her hips forward then drew them slowly back. She moaned then caught her bottom lip between her teeth. "I am."

And what shots they were, too. He fumbled behind her for the clasp to her bra and she followed, easily releasing hooks and allowing the material to slide from her breasts. David hungrily fastened his lips over one rosy tip, then moved impatiently to the other, unable to get enough of her.

Especially when she rocked again.

With an almost inhuman groan, he edged from the chair, and with a single sweep of his arm, cleared the coffee table. Empty beer bottles, food wrappings and candlesticks clicked to the area rug one after another. In one smooth move, he laid her across the smooth surface, sliding her down until her sweet little bottom was even with the end, all the while keeping the connection with her, reveling in the feel of her surrounding him. Taking him in. Making him hers. Her hands moved so quickly he could barely keep track of them, much less identify the myriad sensations they awakened. From his hair where she tugged on the sensitive strands, to his back where she drew her short nails down the length of his burning flesh, to his butt, where she squeezed then pulled him closer at the same time that she thrust her hips upward.

Damn. Her impatient, carnal, needy movements nearly shoved him straight over the edge.

Hooking his arm under the back of her knee, he drew her leg up, pleased with her agility, and wild with desire as she not only happily took every inch of his deep thrust, but sweetly swiveled her hips to take him in even deeper. Needing to get a handle on himself, he slowly began to withdraw. But her whimper and the answering grinding of her hips would have none of it, so instead he filled her.

And oddly felt something begin to fill him instead of the other way around. It began in his chest. More than just the pressurized building of an incredible orgasm, it seemed to spread with every beat of his heart. Heat, surety, peace...

Then Kelli cried out and that peace imploded, like a window bowing inward, then cracking and scattering into crystalline pieces on the other side. Pieces that swirled up and up until they were out of sight in the dark night sky.

"Wow," Kelli murmured, moments later, their bodies spent, their ragged breathing losing its edge.

David budged his head from where it rested against her smooth collarbone, a grin easing across his face. "Yeah. Wow."

7

THE FOLLOWING afternoon Kelli still felt...gob-smacked, wowed, completely out of sorts. As though the world didn't make sense anymore, somehow. As though David had gripped the proverbial rug that she had so safely stood on for the past twenty-five years and effectively yanked it out from under her feet. More than that, he held the battered old familiar rug up bullfighter style, teasing her with it, mocking her. She groaned at the image, practically hearing him say "olé."

Considering that she was in the middle of launching her undercover assignment as the new sales girl at Adult Indulgences, her mind should be everywhere else but on David. But the owner, Jeremy Price, had left her alone in his office to go find something, and her mind kept wandering back to the night before.

While things between her and David had begun on the coffee table, they certainly hadn't ended there. She'd thought the first time had been aberration. A momentary lapse of good sense brought on by the excitement of finally being home. She imagined the incredible passion had been heightened by her new sense of power, of plans nearing completion.

Oh, how very wrong she'd been.

Well, at least partially. She didn't think she was ready to grant David more than just a smidgen of credit for her reaching orgasm not once, not twice, but a whopping three times. She pressed her palm against her burning cheeks. But she had to admit that the guy was...incredible. Attentive. Pleasingly hungry. And he definitely got an A for endurance. But she was nowhere near prepared to admit that her unusual responsiveness was due solely to him.

She tucked a strand of heavily moussed, teased hair behind her ear, searching for alternative explanations. Answers that didn't include David McCoy's bragging smile.

Lack of sex. No, no, lack of really good sex. For years she had voluntarily stood back and watched Bronte conquer the sexual world, all the time wondering at its appeal. Even during her time with Jed she had distantly wondered if that was all there was. Now she knew it wasn't.

That was it. She latched onto the lame rationalization with both hands. She was a woman who had just gone too long without.

She mentally cringed. That was such a man-thing to say.

Still, she couldn't help wondering in a shadowed, cowardly corner of her mind why David sought her out. Certainly he had better things to do than hang around outside her apartment door all day. A guy didn't come by the nickname Stationhouse Casanova for pulling little stunts like that.

She forced the thought from her mind, not willing to go there just yet. She had enough emotional fodder to chew on for the next two years, at least.

Speaking of bullheaded men, her father intruded on her thoughts. She'd picked up the phone no less than four times throughout the day only to hang it back up. Once she'd gotten all the way to the last number. But ultimately she couldn't go through with it. She couldn't help thinking that her making the first call would be akin to apologizing, and she didn't think she had anything to apologize for. If anyone should be apologizing, it should be him. But her own phone—when she hadn't had it off the hook—had stayed criminally quiet.

She shifted uneasily on the simple office chair. At any rate, she really shouldn't be thinking of either of the men currently complicating her life, not when she had a job to concentrate on. She gave a secretive look around.

Who knew there were so many different sex toys?

Although it was the second time in as many days that Kelli had been in the store that catered to sexual tastes obviously far more decadent than hers, she still couldn't take in enough of everything surrounding her. Even sitting in the office chair, she craned her neck to look through the open door. One wall was covered entirely with X-rated videos. Another, with row upon row of leather paraphernalia that looked cruel even for a pet store.

An image of David slipped through her mind and she fought a decidedly naughty shiver.

"Found them," Jeremy Price, the store's owner, said breezing back into the room. And breezing was the word for it. His sexual orientation was blatantly obvious, making her decidedly more comfortable around him. "Just sign there and we're good to go." He placed a W-2 form in front of her.

Kelli smiled at him. Jeremy was an unexpected surprise. And, she hoped, a friendly ally during the time she was assigned to work undercover at Adult Indulgences. She had no cause to think otherwise. Everything else was going as planned, right to the letter. The regular girl, Ginger Olsen, had accepted a generous cash donation to her favorite foundation—herself—and had been given a two-week Jamaican cruise, just to make sure she didn't run through the money and show up at the shop looking for her job back while Kelli was still working undercover. Kelli, herself, had applied for the job the day before. Then undercover task force officers had sidetracked every woman they pegged as applying for the job the second before she could walk through the glass-paned door.

Kelli's own past experience had helped. She'd worked at mall clothing stores during the summers when she was in high school, and had made it to manager of the juniors department in a swanky department store in the two years before she entered the academy.

Throw in a sham recently failed relationship during which

she wasn't required to work, and she was probably overqualified for the position of cashier at the tawdry adult bookstore.

She signed the form with a flourish she was sure was more in fitting with her new persona, then handed it back to Jeremy across the desk of the backroom office.

"That's it then," he said with a dramatic sigh, then smiled. "Welcome to Adult Indulgences."

"Thank you. You won't be disappointed," Kelli fairly purred, barely recognizing her own voice.

Jeremy put the paperwork aside, then stood, coming around the desk. "Let me show you off, kitty cat."

Kelli had stuck with her own name, so she was sure he was merely using the nickname kindly. She managed a smile and slowly got up, wobbling on the too-high high heels, forcing herself to stop plucking at the too-short skirt, and shoving her chest out to distract any passersby from both.

She could do this. She could. If only her father's voice would get out of her head. And if only she could stop thinking about exactly what one Officer David McCoy was doing right about now.

"Jose, come over here," Jeremy called, waving to a guy in his mid-twenties who was stocking newer magazines on a rack. "I want you to meet the latest addition to our little family." The Latino fiddled with the edges of his mustache, then lumbered over, very much like a male cat on the prowl for Kelli's Kitty Cat.

"*Ola, chica,*" he said with a sneaky grin that made Kelli's skin crawl.

"*Ola* yourself," she said, thrusting out an arm covered with beads and metal bracelets. "I'm Kelli."

Jeremy clucked his tongue, then stood back and looked her over. From the tips of her black boots, to the scalloped edge of her too-tight tank, his gaze lingered on every inch. "Not anymore you're not, babe. You've just been promoted." He took a magazine from Jose and rolled it up tightly. Tapping her lightly on the head, he said, "I now officially pronounce you to be Kitty Kat, with two k's." He laughed then slapped the magazine back into Jose's palm. "Doesn't she just look good enough to eat, Jose?"

A snort that Kelli took to mean agreement was Jose's response.

"Okay, then," Jeremy said with another long sigh, then waved his hands. "Let me show you around."

A half hour later Kelli was afraid her eyeballs would fall to the floor. Either that or she would trip over her jaw. From the viewing booths in the back of the shop, to the various classifications of video—from soft porn to hard core—to learning the names of all the sex toys, she felt like her head was going to explode. Her reaction wasn't just from having to memorize each item, but from the crowbar that had just been used to expose her mind to a completely different side of life she had no idea existed. Well, okay, she'd had an idea. She'd even worked undercover twice as a prostitute in New York. But even during those assignments, the second she got the john to name a price, she'd slapped her cuffs on faster than he could blink, so that didn't really count.

Now...well, now she would have to use words she wasn't even sure she knew the meaning of on a daily basis.

"Eighty-three percent of our clientele is from perfectly normal suburbia," Jeremy was telling her as he showed her how to work the cash register.

"And the other seventeen?"

The register bell rang and released the cash drawer. Jeremy jabbed a finger toward the back booths. "Are back there right now."

Kelli laughed, wondering what her duties were in regards to the booths. She cleared her throat. "I won't, you know, have to do any cleanup—"

"Oh, no," Jeremy said, squeezing her shoulder. "Jose gets that job." His smile widened. "We don't want one of those guys pulling you in there, now, do we?" His gaze skimmed her backside. "We want you out here to do what you're designed to do, girlfriend. Get customers to buy, buy, buy."

DAVID COMPARED the address written on his pad to the storefront across the way. Adult Indulgences. In a fashionable part of town, looking no more out of place than the locksmith next to it. Brick facade, white trimmed windows. People walking by, in and out, going about their business as if passing by or browsing through an adult bookstore were a normal part of their day. And perhaps it was. Just because it wasn't part of his lifestyle, didn't mean it wasn't the norm. What passed for normal these days was anything from tongue-piercings and purple hair to self-mutilation and tattoos.

He scratched his chin, trying to imagine his brother Jake in the leather getup the man who just walked out of the place had on. For all he knew his other brother Mitch got into his wife's lacy underwear under his jeans.

The thought made him burst out laughing. If it was one thing he was sure of, it was that he and all four of his brothers—and his father for that matter—were as arrow-straight as they came. Hell, they had a hard enough time with the normal, head-on type of stuff, let alone the strange fetishes this place catered to. None of them had a single tattoo or a piercing. And women's underwear...well, that's what women wore, not men. Certainly not men from the McCoy clan.

He got out of the car and watched a woman who looked not unlike Kelli walk into the place. Hey, to each his own. So long as it didn't hurt anyone else, more power to them. Whatever got your rocks off.

He grimaced at the nonsensical stream of clichés drifting through his mind. Who was he kidding? This stuff made him nervous as hell. He'd sooner go browse through a New Age shop, have his palm read, wear some sort of vampire-repelling crystal around his neck then go into this place.

But if anything were impetus enough, seeing that Kelli was all right certainly was. He didn't know what strings the guys in the task force had had to pull to get her in there, but if there was one place one very innocent looking Kelli Hatfield didn't belong, it was here—no matter how uninnocent her actions the night before.

It took some doing to get the address of the place. So hush-hush was this assignment, he'd had to give up Christmas Eve to work a shift for the guy who had given him the info. The information had only made him that much edgier. Who was watching Kelli? What kind of surveillance was set up on the place? Did she have on a mike? Was there video? How about backup? Even he, with his bad track record with partners, understood that you needed good backup at all times. But Jennings had refused him anything more than the name of the shop she was working at and her hours.

"Stop your stalling, McCoy, and get in there," he mumbled under his breath.

Looking both ways, he tucked his chin into his leather jacket—the only thing he had he deemed suitable for such a visit—and crossed the street.

He opened the door, setting off a digital bell that chimed out. Then hearing the sound of the store's background music, he groaned. Was that really Rod Stewart's "Do You Think I'm Sexy"? He nearly turned tail and ran right there. It was one thing to proclaim yourself a lady-killer, quite another to have to go somewhere to study the stuff. If any of his brothers caught him in this place, he'd be dead meat.

And if Kelli *was* under surveillance, his hide would be Kowalsky's.

He dipped his chin down a little farther into his jacket, then reached up and pulled the side of his plain brown skull cap down to cover his ears.

A woman of forty something walked by him on her way out, shooting him a furtive glance. Why was she looking at him like he was the bad guy? She was the one doing her shopping in the local S&M place.

He glanced down the left side of the shop. It looked just like a family video rental store. He began to relax a little. Until he nearly tripped over a box that held an inflatable woman and it began making moaning noises. He reached down to find the off button, but the moaning only got louder. He dropped the box back to the floor and scooted it under a rack with his foot.

Suddenly, he was altogether too hot. It was all he could do not to turn and run back outside into the cold.

"Can I help you, sir?"

David would recognize Kelli's voice anywhere. Damn. He'd wanted a few minutes to himself to case the joint, then watch her without her knowing he was there. So much for plans.

He cleared his throat and purposely lowered it, keeping his head turned away. "Just lookin'," he said gruffly.

There was a heartbeat of a silence, then she sighed. "All right then. If you need anything, I'll be right over by the cash register."

David didn't dare turn until he heard the click, click of her heels walking away. When he did finally turn, he had to do a double take.

Naw...

There was no way on God's green earth that the woman walking away from him was his partner, Kelli Hatfield. Slack-jawed, he watched feet, clad in shiny patent leather boots, lazily move one in front of the other. The tantalizing stretch of leg from the top of the boots to the bottom of her short-short hem were clad in white fishnet stockings, complete with a line down the back. And the skirt. Woooweee! It was enough to send any man to his knees begging for a chance to peek under it.

No, the woman walking away from him was definitely not his partner. But she did resemble the woman he was coming to know between the sheets.

"Jesus, Kelli, is that you?" he croaked.

KELLI TURNED so quickly, she nearly fell off her heels and straight into the edible underwear stand.

"David!"

What was *he* doing there?

Realizing she had practically shouted his name, she looked around to see who had overheard. The only one within speaking distance was a twenty-something guy looking over the latest edition of *Naked Women Weekly*. So caught up was he in the centerfold, he didn't even glance their way.

When she turned back around, she found David practically gaping at her cleavage. She felt the incredible urge to cover herself.

Funny, she'd spent the past three hours in the shop practicing her sashay, working a little southern drawl into her voice, and trying not to choke at the items the customers laid on the check-out counter. But one look at David and she was ready to run screaming to the closest sporting goods store for a set of the baggiest jogging suits they sold.

Kelli descended on him. "What in the hell are you doing here, McCoy?" She grabbed his arm, ignoring the way the cool soft leather felt against her palm as she spun him toward the door. "And where did you get that ridiculous hat?"

As if in a daze, he slowly reached up and dragged it from his head. Kelli inwardly groaned, suppressing the desire to tell him to put it back on. All that golden blond hair tempted her touch even more than the soft leather under her fingertips.

His mouth worked, but no words came out. She didn't flatter herself into thinking she was the one solely responsible for his speechlessness. Kelli snatched her hand back from tempting territory, then faced him, her hands planted firmly on her leather-clad hips. "What is it, McCoy? Spit it out, man."

"You...you..."

She nodded. "I..."

"You...look...incredible."

Heat swept over Kelli from her cheeks to her toes. She'd been visibly ogled by at least a dozen men that evening, but those few, simple, choked out words made her feel sexy as all get out.

"You didn't answer my question," she pointed out.

His frown told her he wasn't following her.

"What are you, hearing impaired? I asked what...are... you...doing...here?" She slid another glance behind her to make sure Jeremy was nowhere in sight. "And you better make it good, McCoy."

"You weren't at home," he said.

"And..."

It seemed to take everything in his power to rip his gaze from her chest. He concentrated instead on a nearby rack of novels with pink labels plastered all over them warning of sexually explicit material. Kelli could virtually see every ounce of his usual cockiness reassert itself, much as mercury fills a thermometer. When he turned back to her, his big-headed grin was firmly in place, and he seemed to have undergone a demeanor transplant. Where he was awkward and gawking mere moments before, now he was downright sexy, his feet placed apart, his weight leaning on one leg, his gaze openly sweeping her. The warmth that Kelli felt moments before ignited into a full-fledged fire.

"Hey, it's fate, baby cakes." He picked up a magazine. "I happen to come in here all the time. Ask anybody."

Kelli wanted to sock him one. But when he opened the magazine and got a gander at what it held, he instantly dropped it. She laughed and bent over to sweep the magazine up, only afterward realizing how much she'd probably just revealed from behind. She tugged at the unwieldy material. "Uh-huh. Come here all the time, do you?" She showed him the cover of the magazine then slipped it back into its holder. "I happen to know that your appetite is for women, McCoy."

He said something under his breath that sounded like, "You got that right."

She crossed her arms under her breasts, very aware that the action accentuated her cleavage all the more. She refused to think about last night. Refused to remember how he had thoroughly explored every inch of the flesh he was now visually devouring. His being there was distracting enough without her mind delving into areas she had yet to make sense out of.

As expected, his gaze zoomed in immediately on her chest. So long as he talked to her breasts, she could handle him. "Tell me the truth. What are you really doing here?"

"Making sure you're okay."

The urge to pop him one returned full force. The guy was infuriating. "Officially or unofficially?"

His gaze skittered up to her face.

"That's what I thought." She started to turn him toward the door again.

"Look, Hatfield, I know I wasn't exactly...discreet just now. But we've got to talk. Promise we'll talk and I'll leave."

"You've already had your say, McCoy." In fact, he'd already had more than his say, and so had she. And the topic of discussion had nothing to do with her being assigned to the task force. "You're going to leave—"

He leaned in toward her ear, cutting off her words as efficiently as if he'd kissed her. And she found she wanted him to do just that, no matter how unbecoming. His warm breath tickled the skin of her neck. "If you promise to have this talk, I promise I'll leave without blowing your cover," he said, underscoring his point by flicking his tongue over her skin then blowing on it.

Kelli's eyes widened. "You wouldn't!" she whispered harshly.

His grin was back full force. "Try me." He crossed his own arms. "It would be all too easy, Kell. Hell, I didn't think you had what it took to wear a uniform. This whole thing...well, I don't think I have to tell you how much happier I'd be if I got your sexy little bottom fired right here and now."

Kelli could do little more than sputter, upset by his words, turned on by the feel of his mouth so very close to her skin.

"Is there something you need help with, Kitty Kat?" Jeremy asked somewhere behind her.

Kelli leaned back to stare into David's questioning face. He arched a brow and mouthed, "Kitty Kat?" She began slowly shaking her head, as much for David's sake as for Jeremy.

"No, I've got everything under control, Jeremy, thanks."

She sensed he hadn't left. A moment later, he said, "Are you sure?"

"Positive. This...gentleman was just saying how much he liked my perfume. Wants to buy some for his...um, girlfriend. I was just helping him out, that's all."

"All right. But make sure he buys something here before you go sending him off to another store, you hear?"

Kelli laughed and noticed David did, too. She almost slumped against him with relief when she heard the office door close behind her boss.

"Well," David hummed. "I guess I don't have to worry about anything going on between you and the boss now, do I?"

Kelli pushed at him with both hands. "You really take the cake, McCoy, do you know that?"

"Nope. But I'd like to." He ran his rough palm up the back of her net-clad legs and this time she did slump against him.

"You've already had a little too much cake."

"Uh-uh, Kitty Kat. I've merely sampled the icing. I plan to dig a little, um, deeper the next time we're together, so just put those claws away and stop spitting at me."

She groaned, thinking she'd have to make sure they weren't alone again together in this lifetime.

The smile hovering around his luscious lips made her lick her own. "Look at you. You're flustered. Tell me something,

Hatfield? If you can't handle little ol' me, how are you going to protect yourself against a marauding murderer?"

She told him to go do something that was physically impossible, causing him to laugh. "Only if you promise to help." He let her go then looked around the place. "With everything I'm sure you'll pick up around here, I think you're just the person for the job."

Instead of her turning him toward the door, he instead swiveled her to face the cashier's desk. "Now, go on and get back to work. We wouldn't want you to get into any trouble now, would we?" He patted her firmly on the backside and she gasped and stumbled a couple of steps away. "Just remember we need to have that talk."

Talk. Why was Kelli getting the impression there wouldn't be many coherent words included in that little discussion?

She hurried back behind the counter and made busy with her hands, though she did nothing. Her gaze kept straying to where David had unzipped his coat and stepped to the opposite side of the store. She appreciated the curve of his bottom in jeans even as her own still smarted a bit from his swat. She watched him pick up something with his index finger and thumb as if it might bite. She couldn't help herself. She called out, "You break it, you buy it," causing him to nearly drop the sex toy.

She gave a husky little laugh, then smiled at a woman who approached her with her purchases. Kelli tried to concentrate on her rather than her choices. With light brown hair, thirty-ish and petite, she was similar in age, appearance, and class to the other victims. Though none of the D.C. Degenerate, now D.C. Executioner, women had actually been found to have frequented Adult Indulgences, the task force director had thought it important the shop be covered just the same. Kelli rang up the items, then completed the transaction. Sheesh, she could easily have run into the woman at any number of places. The hairdresser's. The grocery store. The doctor's office. If not for this assignment, she'd have happily lived the rest of her life not knowing what really went on behind the closed doors of these perfectly normal-looking people.

Let's face it. Who really needed bottles of flavored oils in order to have a good time? Her gaze automatically flicked back to David and her throat closed. Not her, that's for sure. Time—more specifically, two times—had proven she needed little more than privacy, fresh air and David McCoy.

"Those are on sale," the woman pointed out as Kelli rang up a pair of red silk panties edged with black lace.

"Are they?" Kelli searched them for a tag to find they were missing half the fabric. "Um, how much?"

The woman quoted a price and Kelli entered it, not up to going back there and fingering through the rack to make sure the woman was right. Not so much because she was appalled by the lingerie, but because for that price she was tempted to pick up a pair for herself.

She bagged the purchases and handed them to the customer. "Don't do anything I wouldn't do," she said with a saucy smile.

"I won't."

If you only knew...

Without someone to keep her occupied, she switched her attention again to David. Now that a bit of time separated his closeness from her highly David-sensitive nerves, her spine began to stiffen. What did he mean by her not being fit for a uniform? Sure, maybe he'd been floored when she not only showed up at the station for work the day after their encounter, but ended up being his partner, but what made him think he was capable of judging her competency as a cop? And this time it hadn't sounded as if his conclusions had been drawn on her merely being female. They sounded as though they were based on specific knowledge about her.

"How would you know what I'm capable of," she said under her breath.

Then it hit her. There was one area that he was privy to exactly how competent she was. In bed.

Her cheeks flamed.

Oh God...

Was he basing his judgment on how well she had...how much she knew...how good she was...?

She groaned out loud, earning her his attention. She quickly turned away. Sure, maybe she wasn't all that experienced when it came to the bedroom. But that didn't mean she was innocent, for cripe's sake. And her inexperience with sex had absolutely nothing to do with how savvy she would be on the job. She fully intended to have that detective's shield by the time she turned thirty, no two ways about it.

Her ability to do that, however, rested a whole lot on how well she performed in this assignment.

The guy who had been ogling the new issues rack of magazines sauntered up to the counter.

"Hey, sweet thing, how come I don't see any pictures of you in these?" he asked, his gaze slithering down her scantily clad body.

She was aware without even looking that David was tuned into their conversation. No matter how slimy the guy's attention made her feel, she pasted on a smile and leaned suggestively across the counter. "Do you really think I make the grade?"

"Oh, yeah, baby, you definitely make the grade." He put his choices down on the counter.

She batted her eyelashes. "Too bad I don't have a portfolio or anything, huh?" She began ringing up the magazines.

"You talking pictures?"

"Uh-huh."

His flashy grin broadened. "Well, hell, why didn't you say so? I'd be more than happy to snap a few, um, photos, you know, for good will's sake."

A hand came from out of nowhere, clutching the guy by the

collar of his sheepskin coat. "If there are any pictures to be taken, you can bet I'll be the one taking 'em, slimeball," David said, fairly growling at the other man.

"And who are you?"

Kelli smiled at him innocently. She hadn't been sure how David would react, but she admitted to being slightly pleased that he had.

"I'm the guy she's going to marry."

Both of her eyebrows shot up so high they were probably lost in her hairline. Had he just said what she thought he had?

The guy held up his hands in surrender. "Whoa, buddy. I wasn't asking the girl to marry me, if you get my drift. But if she's claimed property, I don't want nothing to do with it, you know?"

"Claimed property?" Kelli repeated.

"Uh-huh," David said with a grin, finally releasing the guy.

Kelli rolled her eyes toward the ceiling. From lady-killer to old woman in one blink of an eye. Despite the beef her father had with the McCoys, she suspected he and David would get along famously. After all, they shared the exact same view on her capabilities, which lay somewhere between zip and zero.

The customer straightened his coat. "If you're ever interested in sharing some of those pictures, I'd pay a couple of bucks for them."

Kelli gasped, then leaned across the counter to where David was cocking his arm back. "Don't even think about it."

She quickly accepted the guy's money then apologized as she saw him out the door.

"Looks like you're really not interested in having that conversation you were talking about," she swiveled toward David and squashed the pads of her index finger and thumb together. "Because you just came this close to getting me fired already. And it's only my first day on the job."

"That guy was—"

"That guy was someone I could handle, thank you very

much." She tilted her head to the side. "You seem to forget that we went through the same exact training at the academy, Mc-Coy."

"Yeah, but learning something and putting it into use are two entirely different things."

"Marry?" she blurted, choosing to ignore his comment.

Rather than looking away as she expected, he had the audacity to grin. "Yeah. Pretty good comeback, don't you think?"

She groaned, rounded him, then forcefully pushed him toward the door. "Get out of here, McCoy. Before I show you just how well I can put to use what I learned at the academy."

"Academy?" a male voice echoed from behind her.

Kelli tensed, as did David's back muscles through his coat. She plucked her hands from him, then messed with her skirt while she turned to face Jeremy. *Think, Hatfield, think.* "Yes, the academy," she said around an affected smile. "You know. The Holy Mother's Academy for Girls? That's the high school I attended."

Jeremy grinned. "A Catholic girl, huh? Ooo, you're just getting more and more interesting, Kitty Kat." His gaze switched to take in David. He made no secret of his open appreciation for the prime piece of male flesh. It was all Kelli could do not to claim *him* as her property. "Well, aren't you going to introduce us?"

"Of course," Kelli said quickly. "Jeremy, this is...David Mc-Coy."

"Well, hello and how do you do, David McCoy." The shop owner extended his hand and David hesitantly took it. "It's not often we get guys of your...caliber in here. Have you ever thought about modeling? You'd be to-die-for in one of those little leather getups over there." He tapped his finger against his pursed lips. "Without the hood, though. We wouldn't want to cover up those finely chiseled features."

Kelli recognized a smoother version of the come-on line the last customer had just tried on her, and cringed. She slanted a gaze at David, unsure of his reaction. She was surprised to find him grinning at Jeremy. "If that was a compliment, thank you."

Jeremy chuckled. "Oh, you are priceless."

"I'm also Kelli's fiancé."

Kelli yearned to stomp her high heel on top of David's foot with every ounce of energy she possessed. "*Ex*-fiancé," she said, scrambling to save the situation. Didn't the idiot know that part of her cover was that she had just come off a long relationship?

The two men fell silent, leaving her to wonder whether or not her knee-jerk reaction had been particularly wise. Or if David had completely screwed up everything before it had even begun.

"For now. But I wouldn't count on that status holding for long," David said, his voice akin to a soft hum.

Jeremy sighed, then chuckled good-naturedly. "Ah, why is it women always get the best men?" he asked, then sighed. He waved his hand dismissively. "Never mind." He eyed David one more time. "It was nice meeting you...Mr. McCoy. Given your connection to our Kitty Kat here, I hope that means we'll be seeing more of you."

David's grin was wider than she'd ever seen it. She braced herself for his response. "On that, you can count, Jeremy."

The owner nodded in agreement, then went back into his office.

Kelli glared at David.

"So," he said, "what's say we meet back at your place later?"

"No."

He quirked a brow. "My place?"

"Never." This time she made no attempt to physically remove him from the shop. She allowed her expression to speak for her. "Get this straight, McCoy. I don't need you hovering over me under the pretense of protecting me." She crossed her arms, but this time there was nothing provocative about the move. "I don't need you thinking that just because we've slept together—"

"Twice," he added.

She rolled her eyes. "It doesn't give you the right to come and go as you please. And I certainly don't need you screwing up my assignment." She had promised herself she wouldn't touch him, but she couldn't resist poking her finger into his rock solid chest. A move that may have knocked her off track a few minutes ago, but she was so angry a bulldozer probably couldn't have moved her at that moment. "And don't even joke about blowing my cover, McCoy. I'll go to the task force and Kowalsky so fast you won't know what hit you. And I think they'll be even less amused than I am with your interfering behavior." She narrowed her eyes. "And I don't think I have to remind you who my father is, now, do I?" She really hated throwing that extra bit in, but hey, all was fair, right?

"I'm—"

"Don't." She stopped him with a raised hand.

"But—"

"Stop."

"Still—"

"Forget about it, McCoy. Absolutely nothing you could say to me right now could make me think about anything else but watching your butt, no matter how cute, walk straight through that door forever."

He heaved a sigh. "You'd really make me lose my job?"

She winced but held herself straight. "Let's put it this way. I care as much about your job security as you care about mine."

"Ouch."

She pointed to the door. "Now get out of here."

8

DAVID DRIBBLED the basketball the length of the indoor court, weaving in and out, skirting around the teenagers he coached at the youth center downtown. Several of them were already taller than he was, and far more talented, but tonight he had an edge they couldn't hope to challenge. Tonight wasn't normal practice or game night, but he'd been restless and distracted and had come anyway to find most of his team there, preferring the warmth and companionship of the center to the bitter December cold outside. Sneakers squealed against the waxed old wood, sweat dripped from his chin, and thankfully for the first time in days he wasn't focused solely on one sexy Kelli Hatfield.

He drew to a quick stop and set up his shot...and missed the hoop by a mile.

So much for focusing on something other than that maddeningly sensual woman. Even when he didn't want her to be, she was there on the fringes of his thoughts, her luscious mouth smiling, her green eyes snapping, her bare back arching. It had been even worse recently, since all attempts to see her in the past two days had been effectively blocked.

He'd known his showing up at the shop the other night had irritated her, but he hadn't known he'd so thoroughly pissed her off. He was still trying to figure that one out. Why did his wanting to protect her send her off the mental deep end? Hell, his experience with women was that he didn't pay enough attention to them. Essentially Kelli was accusing him of paying her too much attention.

It didn't make any sense.

After she'd hung up in his ear the day before, he thought it prudent to give her a little time to cool off. While thoughts of her at that damn store, unprotected, drove him up the wall, thoughts of her slamming the door on any further contact between them were even more frustrating.

Yeah. He'd lay low for a couple of days, wait for everything to blow over, then show up at her place begging for forgiveness.

If only he knew what he would be apologizing for.

Chris Tucker, a fifteen-year-old who was already a foot taller than he was, lumbered up to walk him to the mostly empty bleachers. "That one should have been all yours, coach. What happened?"

David fished a towel from his gym bag and dragged it across his face. "Wasn't focusing, Tuck. It's as simple as that."

The kid grinned, likely finding it funny that he could use some of his own coaching advice. "Yeah."

David waved him away. "You go on and I'll watch. This old guy has had enough for one night."

Chris didn't believe him for a minute, but thankfully he didn't say anything. He rejoined the other kids on the court, which included two females, and then continued play.

Normally David made it a point to keep up with the teens. It was a good way to keep in shape, burn off the excess energy usually left after a long and frustrating day, as well as help some neighborhood kids keep off the corner. Not just one specific corner, but all of them. Everywhere where deals were made, drugs sold, young flesh peddled. He'd started coaching five years ago and planned to continue doing it until he could no longer physically keep up. He was determined that would be never.

He dropped to the first bench and watched the kids work their way to the opposite end of the court. Even as he did, their images faded to be superimposed with the mental image of

Kelli Hatfield. He grimaced. The mere thought of her working in that place, with all those losers slobbering all over her, dressed like... He went brain dead just thinking about the close-fitting, downright sexy clothes she'd had on. The boots alone filled his mind with fantasies of seeing her wearing them, and nothing else, standing over him as he lay stretched out on her bed.

"Hey, little bro, how's it hanging?"

David turned to where the spot on the bleachers one up from him was no longer vacant. "Fine, couldn't be better," he said by rote, his token response for the past couple of days when he was everything but fine.

Marc McCoy hiked a skeptical brow as he laid his coat on the bench beside him.

David chugged down a swallow of bottled water, the cold liquid barely sliding its way past his tight throat. "How did you know to find me here?"

Marc shrugged. "Lucky guess. If you weren't at home or in Manchester, it was a pretty good bet that you'd be here."

David gave him a meaningful glance. "With Melanie about to pop that baby of yours, I would have thought you'd be chained to her side."

He had to do a double take. Had his brother actually just frowned? Uh-oh, was there trouble in paradise?

"Haven't you heard? She's staying out at the house. What with the lame duck still on Penn Ave, and the president-elect primed to take over next month, we've all been putting in double shifts. Mel's fit to be tied."

"Ah, life in the Secret Service." David messed around with the valve on his bottle. Maybe this women-problems thing was due to something in the water. "You think hanging out with me is going to help matters any?" he asked.

Marc shrugged. "What Mel doesn't know, won't hurt her. Besides, I need to unwind a little before making the long drive out to Manchester." He grabbed the water bottle and took a swallow. "Don't tell her I said this, but I personally think she's jealous. She just wishes she could be out there scoping out potentials right along with me. This baby thing has her wound up just as tight as I am."

David smiled. "Yeah, you're probably right."

"So what's up with you?"

He shrugged. "Not much. Same old same old."

Marc stared at him. "Uh-huh."

"What?"

His brother shook his dark head. "Oh nothing."

From the door in the corner a couple of teenage girls walked in dressed to the neighborhood nines, shaking their heads to rid themselves of the light snow that started falling about an hour ago. Marc sat up a little straighter. "Woooweee, will you get a load of that," he said appreciatively. "They didn't make them that way when I was a teen."

"Yeah, they did. It was just so long ago you can't remember."

Marc slugged him playfully in the arm.

"You just make sure you keep your hands to yourself, you hear? Aside from them being jailbait, there's Mel to think about. You might be able to handle her, but I'm not even going to chance facing her wrath."

Marc rubbed the back of his neck. "Hey, it's just eye candy. You know I'd never act on it."

"Yeah, well, normally you wouldn't even notice."

"A month without some Grade-A sex will do that to a guy. But as soon as the doc gives the thumbs-up, Mel and I are leaving the baby with Michelle and taking off for the weekend to make up for lost time."

David barely heard him.

"That's my story, little bro. Now what's yours?"

"Huh?"

Marc nodded toward the girls who had taken seats down the way. "You're the loverboy with the sweet tooth and you've barely even looked at them. No matter the age, there's just something in your genes that makes you want to win every woman over."

"Yeah, I must have inherited all the charm you guys didn't," he mumbled even as he grimaced at the description. "Not in the mood tonight, I guess."

"You guess." Marc leaned his forearms against his thighs. "Oooh, I recognize that expression."

"What expression?"

Marc pointed at him. "That expression. The one that says you expect the world to end at any minute. Oh, boy, you've got it bad."

He looked away.

"Okay, who is she, and why aren't you with her tonight?"

David blinked at him. Of the five of them, it could never be said that Marc was the most observant. Not when it came to relationships anyway. In fact, Connor relished calling him dumber than a doornail when it came to women. He grimaced. He wondered if they all had been wrong. Marc had been the first of them to marry. It may have taken a baby and an assassin to get him to come around, but he had long before the rest of them.

He considered lying to Marc, telling him that the last thing he had was woman problems, but he figured his brother deserved some credit for his powers of observation, however dubious. "Kelli."

"Kelli," Marc drew out, coaxing him into sharing more.

"Kelli Hatfield. She's my new partner. Well, she was anyway, until she got this special undercover assignment with the Executioner task force."

"Hatfield...Hatfield." Marc pondered along with the kids still playing in front of them. His eyes widened. "Not as in Garth Hatfield?"

David visibly winced. Trust Marc to put two and two together when it had taken him days to add up the sum. "One and the same. She's his only kid."

"Does Pops know?"

David leaned back. "As of right now, there's nothing to know, because nothing's going on."

"But there was."

Was there? David couldn't be sure anymore. If his brother had asked him a couple of days ago, he'd have answered with an unqualified yes. But now... Well, now he wasn't all too sure where he stood with the frustrating woman. She was all soft and sexy on the outside, but inside he was coming to suspect that she was impenetrable steel.

When Marc had said he had it bad, he put his finger directly on his dilemma. He did have it bad for Kelli Hatfield. Which was totally baffling, because he'd never felt quite like this before. And without previous experience under his belt, he had no idea what to do about it. He felt like a mouse running around an unfamiliar maze. He could smell the cheese, he wanted the cheese, but he couldn't find the damn cheese.

Marc chuckled and shook his head. "I never thought I'd live to see the day when a woman would get to you, Casanova."

David bristled. "And why not? I'm human, aren't I? If you cut me, don't I bleed red?"

"Yeah, but up 'til now it was red roses."

"Cute, McCoy, real cute."

Marc stretched his long legs out to rest against the bleacher below him and crossed them at the ankle. "So a woman has gotten the better of the infamous David McCoy, huh?"

"Infamous?" David hiked a brow.

"Come on. Don't tell me you didn't purposely build that naughty reputation you have. Forget Manchester. Forget the M.P.D. You're now a citywide bad boy."

"And you're making much more out of this than there is."

"Am I?" He reached over and picked up his coat, slipping something out of the inside pocket. "Normally I don't read this garbage, but Mel called this morning practically shrieking with the news." He slapped a folded back weekly magazine into David's stomach. "Read it and weep, Casanova Cop."

David stared at the glossy paper, afraid to touch it. Is that how everyone and his brothers really saw him? As some sort of love-'em-and-leave-'em renegade? He groaned and forced himself to pick up the magazine. Spread across the left-hand page was a picture of him in full uniform grinning with his arms crossed. He recognized the background as being just after the hostage situation the other day. On the other page written in bold letters was "Casanova Cop: What D.C. Woman Wouldn't Want to Find Him Under Her Christmas Tree?"

Yeah, every woman but Kelli Hatfield. Especially after she got a look at this story.

He closed his eyes and groaned. He vaguely recognized the reporter's name as someone he talked to after the hubbub. He'd had no idea she'd planned to run this kind of story on him. Then again he hadn't bargained on the news media jumping all over the hostage story either. He'd taken his share of ribbing from fellow officers over the past week, and even the kids had mentioned it before he told them to can it.

Marc pointed to a highlighted part of the story. "I like this part the best. She talks about your being a bad boy in need of a woman's good loving to turn you around."

David groaned even louder, then threw the magazine back at Marc with more force than was necessary.

"Hey, I thought you'd eat up coverage like this."

"A week ago, maybe I would have. But that damn fluff piece probably just cut my chances of getting through to Kelli in half."

Marc laughed and tossed the magazine onto David's gym bag. "I know I'm repeating myself, but I can't help it. I never thought I'd live to see the day when a woman would get the better of you."

David dropped his head into his hands and rubbed his eyes. "I didn't either."

Marc fell silent, leaving only the sounds of the sneakers squeaking against the basketball court, and the good-natured jests of the players.

What was he going to do?

"You'll figure it out," Marc said, as if he'd asked the question aloud. "You're a McCoy and McCoys always get their man. Or woman, in this case." Marc thumped him on the back.

"We're not talking about a fugitive here, Marc."

"Worse. We're talking about the opposite sex." He sat up. "You know, I still have all those, um, women's magazines at home if you want to take a look through them. Not that they ever helped me, but you never know. They have all kinds of crap in there on what a woman really wants from a man." He grinned. "Although given that Casanova Cop piece, apparently you've already got it."

David groaned again. "Shut up, Marc. Just shut up."

KELLI PACED the length of the reversible bulletin board she'd set up in the corner of her dining room, right next to her three-foot live Christmas tree. She methodically searched pictures, diagrams and information posted on nearly every square inch of this side of the board, seeking out something, anything, new, while Kojak alternately watched her and the flashing lights on the tree. Lying a safe distance away so as not to get stepped on, his head resting on his meaty paws, only his eyes shifted. An occasional yawn told her how bored he was with the entire routine.

There had to be something here, something she'd missed three years ago, the last time she'd gone through the copy of the inactive file on her mother's murder. Finding a spot for the slip she held, she pulled out a green pushpin, then fastened the phone message to the corkboard between a studio photograph of her mother taken eighteen years ago, and the media shot of her body being carried out of the house, Kelli's own image as she ran after the sheeted figure carefully cut out.

She tapped the board, causing it to rotate and reveal the side she had mapped out on the D.C. Executioner's crimes, then flipped it back again, the images beginning to swim before her eyes.

"There has to be something...."

Kojak snapped his head up and whined hopefully. She slowly turned her head and zoomed in on him. He seemed to sense that she wasn't really looking at him, rather was looking past him for the answer that always seemed on the edge of her mind. Kojak barked.

"What is it, boy? You think I'm heading in the wrong direction?"

His stubby little tail moved frantically back and forth, indicating his answer in the affirmative.

Kelli flopped down in the dining room chair and fingered through the other material strewn across the surface. Kojak came to her side and she absently dropped her hand and petted him.

"Maybe you're right. Maybe this burning the candle at both ends stuff is finally catching up with me."

She rested her other elbow on the table, then propped up her head with her hand. The past couple of days had been grueling. She began each morning down at task force headquarters, reviewing new information that had come in on the suspect—today it had been two different character profiles and a hazy almost unusable suspect sketch—and turning in her own detailed notes on the case. Then came changing and checking in for the job within a job itself. She'd forgotten how much of a physical drain working the sales floor could be. Heap on top of that her need to note every suspicious character and scope out each potential victim, and by the end of her shift her brain was about ready to explode with details she had to retain until she got home and could make her notes.

Kojak got up and lumbered toward the kitchen. She wearily eyed the files littering the table. She'd finally gone through them when she couldn't sleep two nights ago because images of a certain someone kept slipping through her mind. Since then, she'd spent every free moment following up leads long dropped and dogging trails long gone cold.

She glanced at her watch. She listlessly toyed with the files, then looked at her watch again. It was after ten. As tired as she was, a nice long hot bath, bed and the book lying half open on the nightstand should have sounded awfully tempting. But it didn't. Not when she knew that long periods of time without something to occupy her attention were just inviting trouble in the image of David McCoy. And the romance she was currently reading would only further exacerbate the situation.

She reached for the phone, then pulled her hand back. Bronte had left for New Hampshire that morning to visit her folks for Christmas.

Christmas. Was it really only three days away?

She rubbed her forehead. David wasn't the only man she hadn't talked to recently. Garth Hatfield was proving even more stubborn than she was. She'd given in and called his office phone yesterday and left a brief message. He'd never called back.

Why was life so damn complicated?

Kojak wandered over to sit practically on her foot, making his usual postfeeding sounds.

"That good, huh?" she sighed. "Ah, to have your uncomplicated life."

He barked then began gnawing at something near his back end. Kelli laughed. "Then again...no."

Her thoughts drifted and she was convinced she'd fallen asleep with her eyes open until Kojak whined. She looked down, having to see that her hand rested idly against his ribcage before she realized she'd stopped petting him. She scratched him behind the ears. "What's the matter, Jackie boy?

Feeling a little neglected lately?" His panting seemed to increase in intensity. "Yeah. Me, too."

She pushed back from the table and Kojak instantly got up, too. She eyed him and his bulky frame. "All right, all right, enough with the guilt trip. I'll give you a treat, okay?" He barked, doing the canine equivalent of the rumba as he followed her into the kitchen. "That's treat. Singular. As in one. You got it? And I don't want to hear any complaints. You just ate."

She reached on top of the refrigerator where she had his goodie box stashed and thrust her hand into it. Nothing. The box was empty.

Talk about guilt trips.

"Sorry, buddy, but we're all out of comfort food." He barked. "What? You don't believe me? Take a look for yourself." She held the box out. He sniffed, and sniffed again, then began whining.

"I know how you feel." Boy, did she ever. She was so desperate for the sound of a friendly human voice she was making do by talking to an animal who couldn't answer her.

She dropped the empty box into the garbage, then turned toward the refrigerator itself. Not one thing edible for a human, much less a dog.

She closed the kitchen door, trying to figure out a way to break the news to him. She highly doubted there was a pet supply store open at ten, and that was the only place she could get the brand of special diet treats he would touch.

Then it occurred to her that she knew exactly where she could come by some treats on such short notice. There was this certain someone who took great pride in wooing her dog away from her. She plucked a Post-it Note attached to the refrigerator door with a handcuff magnet, then forced herself to put it back where it was. If she was any kind of modern woman, she'd crumple it up and throw it into the garbage along with the empty treat box. But she wasn't quite ready to do that yet.

She eyed where Kojak had dropped to the floor, the epitome of canine disappointment and depression. Then ignoring the voice telling her it was a big mistake, she said, "Hey, Jack, you wanna go for a walk, boy?"

DAVID EMERGED from the bathroom fastening a towel around his hips. The workout at the basketball court had nicely tired out his muscles but his mind continued irritatingly along on its Kelli Hatfield track. Grimacing, he grabbed the remote, flipping through the channels until he came across a rerun of *The Simpsons*. Recognizing the episode as one of his favorites, he tossed the remote to the two milk crates that served as his coffee table, trying to forget another coffee table he'd recently become very familiar with. Forcing his gaze away, he stalked into the kitchen and grabbed a beer.

Of course whatever physical release of tension he'd gained from the workout on the court was obliterated by his stress-inducing conversation with Marc. Trust his brother to further complicate a situation that was probably pretty simple once you cleared away all the garbage. Standing in front of the open refrigerator door, he gulped down half a beer, then grabbed a half deli sandwich he'd tossed in there when he got home from work.

Ignoring that the towel had slipped a little lower on his hips, he sauntered back into the living room and stared at the television screen. He grinned at something Homer said, then idly wondered if Kelli had ever watched the show. His grin vanished as he took another bite of ham on rye. Kelli probably scoured the proliferation of news shows cramming the network stations, absorbing every byte should she need it to solve a case somewhere down the road.

He reached out and poked a button on the remote, but the talking head failed to keep his interest and he hit the last channel button, instantly relaxing as the cartoon again filled the screen. He took another bite of his sandwich, feeling mustard trickle down the side of his mouth.

A brief knock sounded at the door. He glanced at his waterproof watch, then swiped at the spot of mustard. "Jeff's one door down," he called out.

On his worst days, he was tempted to run his neighbor in for disturbing the peace. But he never did. Jeff was a popular guy who had a lot of friends who just happened to stop by at all times of the day and night. He was used to it. That didn't mean, however, that he couldn't be a wee bit envious.

Another knock.

Sighing, David walked to the door, slid his beer into the crook of his arm, then opened it. "I said that Jeff's—" His eyes widened as he stared at the pair waiting in the hall. He couldn't have been more shocked had he opened the door to find Homer Simpson standing there.

Kojak barked, barely contained by the short leash Kelli had him on. He looked at the dog, then back to his owner, certain he was seeing things.

"I know it's late, but Kojak and I were out walking, and, well..." Her words trailed off as her gaze slid the length of his unclothed body. "Oh, God," she said softly, her cheeks blazing the most amazing shade of red.

David stared down at where his towel was barely hanging on, looked at the beer still in the crook of his arm, and the mess of a sandwich in his hand. Remembering the mustard that had dripped down his chin, he swiped at it with the back of his hand, hoping he was rubbing in the right place.

"Hi," he said. "Come in."

"No, I...we're interrupting you. I think we should just go—"

"No!" he fairly shouted, causing her to jump and the towel around his hips to dip even lower. When it would have slid off altogether, he grabbed at the front, holding it tight. "I just got out of the shower and was catching a bite." He grimaced, wondering if he could waste anymore time stating the obvious.

"Why don't you two come in so I can go, um, put something on?"

He turned and led the way in, kicking a pile of sports magazines out of the way as he went. He saw his apartment as she would and mentally cursed himself. Then he mildly cursed her. What was it with this woman? He tries to contact her, she ignores him. The instant he gives up, she pops up on his doorstep when he's at his absolute worst.

The door quietly clicked closed behind her. "K, would you just settle down."

"You can let him loose if you want," he said, setting his beer down on one of the crates. He stopped himself from shoving what was left of the sandwich into his mouth and put it next to the bottle instead. "I'm, um, just going to go put something on. Make yourself at home."

He stepped toward the door to his bedroom. He had it half closed behind him when Kojak darted in.

"Kojak! Get back here."

David popped his head around the door. "I've got him."

Then he closed the door and softly uttered every curse word he'd learned in his thirty-year existence. The dog plunked his rump down on the floor and sat looking at him, his head cocked slightly to the side. "You think this is funny, huh?" He grabbed the blue flannel shirt hanging on the doorknob. He sniffed the underarms, then slipped into it. "Just see if you get any more treats from me."

At the word treat, Kojak barked, causing David to cringe. The building didn't allow pets. All he needed now was a call from the building manager who lived below him to round out a perfectly awful night. "Okay, okay. I was just joking. Give me a second, will ya?"

He reached past the pooch and grabbed the jeans on the bed and hopped into them, only as he began zipping them remembering he hadn't put briefs on. Oh, well. If things were finally going to take an upward turn he wouldn't have his jeans on for long anyway. He carefully zipped them up then craned his neck to see his hair in the mirror across the room. He'd just towel-dried it after his shower and it was sticking up at odd angles all over his head.

"Damn."

A couple of minutes later he walked into the other room, still barefoot, his shirt hanging open, but as presentable as he could swing in five minutes. Kojak followed him out.

Kelli was perched on the arm of the futon. She looked at him, then back at the television, an amused sparkle in her green eyes. David groaned and reached out to shut off *The Simpsons* midjoke. "I, um, just turned it on. I don't watch that stuff," he said.

She smiled. "Uh-huh."

He started to walk toward the kitchen. "Can I get you something? A beer? A soda?"

Her gaze dropped to his chest and the smile faded from her face. "Um, no thanks. I really shouldn't drink and walk and it's kind of late for a sugar and caffeine buzz."

He frowned at her. "Water?"

Her gaze skittered away from him as she nodded. "Okay."

Kojak nudged his head against his knee. "All right then. One water and one treat coming up."

Get it together, man, he told himself once he was out of view in the kitchen. You can handle this.

It wasn't often that he had a woman in his apartment. He rarely gave out his address. But he hadn't thought twice when he'd fastened both his address and his phone number to Kelli's refrigerator a couple of days back. Perhaps because he'd never thought she'd use it. Or maybe because he'd hoped she would.

Either way he felt out of his element here. He'd never once given a second thought about his lifestyle. Never, that is, until Kelli came a-knocking at his door. Now he was wondering if the low pile gray carpet could do with a vacuum, wished he had thought to do the dishes piled up in the sink, and wondered if there was some way to order a new couch and have it delivered in the next half hour.

"Way to impress the woman, McCoy," he said under his breath as he washed out a glass then filled it with ice and tap water. Only as he was walking back into the other room did he manage to remember to grab the box of treats sitting on the counter.

Kojak came running up and he tossed him one. All he needed now was for the overgrown pooch to jump on him and cause him to drop the water.

"There we are," he said, holding the glass out to her where she was still perched anxiously on the arm of his futon.

Was it him or had Kelli just jumped?

He frowned as she took the glass and offered up a soft thanks.

He dropped down to sit on the other side of the sofa. "You can sit down. I won't bite."

She smiled and slowly shifted to sit next to him. "I don't know if I'm convinced of that."

He held up his hands. "Have I ever done anything you didn't want me to?"

She shook her blond head. "No. But this place...well, it's just what I'd expect from the Casanova Cop."

"Saw that, did you?"

"Not that it matters. That's your nickname anyway. I hear it every time I walk into the station. 'Hey, Hatfield, how's that Casanova Cop of yours doing?' I don't even want to know how they found out. Not that I'm claiming you, by the way. And the piece...well, let's just say it's hard to miss. By now they probably have copies posted all over the station."

He groaned inwardly.

"Nice choice of a color for the walls."

He stared at the black paint. "They were that way when I moved in." He shrugged. "Matched the futon, so I left 'em."

"Um-hmm. I especially like your tree."

He winced at the tiny, deformed silver Christmas tree he'd put up on top of the television. It bore a total of four bulbs and half the lights were missing. "What's the matter with it? It's...Christmasy."

He thought about picking up his beer bottle, then dismissed it, instead stretching his arm across the back of the futon. "So..." he said, "you and Kojak were just out for a walk, huh?"

She seemed inordinately fixated on the close proximity of his arm. "What?"

He pulled his arm back. "Okay, Kelli, spill it. What's really going on here?"

9

Kelli blinked at him several times. It was a valid question. What *was* she doing there? The problem was, she really didn't have an answer. Unusual, since she usually had an answer for everything, even if sometimes it didn't make much sense.

She shrugged. "I was out of treats and Kojak looked so miserable..."

That was lame.

"So you walked a mile and a half in the dead of winter in the middle of the night to come over here so your dog could have a treat?"

She smiled at him. "Yeah. Got a problem with that?"

"Hey, if it works for you." He grinned at her, again stretching that arm of his across the back of the sofa. Her gaze flicked to where the action further opened the unbuttoned flaps of his soft flannel shirt. She'd half expected to find his apartment filled to the rim with weights, but as far as she could tell there wasn't even a dumbbell in the place. She idly wondered how he managed to keep in such great shape. He didn't strike her as the fitness club type.

And she was spending far too much time staring at his six-pack abs.

She cleared her throat and sipped at her water when all she really wanted to do was grab his beer bottle and guzzle the rest of the contents down.

"How are things at the station?" she asked idly, cringing at the small talk.

"They're okay. Johnson and I have settled into a pretty good routine."

"And you got a guy this time around. Good for you." She tried to translate his suddenly dark expression.

"How are things at Adult Indulgences?"

She averted her gaze and ran her fingertip along the rim of her glass. "Okay. A little more grueling than I thought."

"Any progress?"

"On what? Catching the D.C. Executioner?" She shook her head. "No. The heads of the task force are starting to get edgy. The deadline between the timing of his previous crimes is coming up and they want to get him before he can strike again."

"Isn't that a bit optimistic?"

"That's what I thought. I mean, they just set up the task force and already they're leaning on the undercover cops to come up with something. This guy has been lurking out there for over three years and they don't have one solid piece of evidence against him, aside from a couple of Average Joe sketches that could be anybody and a DNA workup that doesn't help us until we actually have a suspect." She sighed and put her glass down on the table. "And they expect us to come waltzing in with him in cuffs yesterday."

"It probably doesn't help that the first murder victim was a cousin twice removed of a senator."

She jerked to look at him. "How do you know that?"

He shrugged a little too nonchalantly. "Word gets around the division. You know that."

"Yeah, but that little piece of info was being kept hush-hush."

David grinned. "There's no such thing as hush-hush in this city, Kelli. If information can be used, it will be. I've heard of guys who make a living out of selling bits to the local news media."

She shook her head and tried to settle back into the cushion, then immediately sat back up when her back made contact with the crook of his arm. She nearly leapt off the couch when he touched her shoulder.

"You're wound up tighter than a fishing reel."

She tried to shrug him off. "I came over here because I needed some human company, McCoy, not because I was looking to get laid."

"It might be a good outlet for the tension radiating from you."

"So might a good sock in the kisser."

He threw his handsome head back and laughed. "Good point." While his mouth said one thing, his fingers were still kneading the tight muscles of her shoulders. She tried to shrug him away again.

"Would you just relax?"

"I can't," she blurted.

He narrowed his eyes. "Hey, Hatfield, even I know the meaning of the word no. This isn't an attempt to get you out of those jeans, no matter how good the wares underneath look. This is just a friend helping a friend."

"A friend helping a friend," she whispered. How much she wanted that now. A friend. Someone to talk about all her worries to.

Kelli drew in a deep breath and closed her eyes, trying to imagine Bronte's innocent touch affecting her this way.

Taking her response as a go-ahead, David slightly shifted her so her back was to him. Then he eased a path down her back with both hands as if testing the muscles there.

"Ouch," she said when he probed a little too thoroughly near her neck.

"Shhh."

She obeyed, noticing as his probing touch changed into a soft, relaxing one. She heard Kojak yawn and cracked open her eyes to find him curling into prime sleep position near the door, either bored stiff by the lack of action, or tired out from the long walk. She smiled, somewhere in the recesses of her mind thinking it interesting he should be so comfortable here, in David's apartment.

"Kelli?"

She hummed her response, finding it amazing that a man as rough and tough as David McCoy could have hands so incredibly gentle.

"What's really bothering you?"

She snapped upright.

"Don't do that. You just undid five minutes of work."

She immediately tried to make herself relax again, but her muscles weren't having any of it.

She shrugged as he kneaded a particularly nasty knot in her right shoulder. "I don't know. Are there ever times when you think that if just one more thing happens you're afraid you'll run screaming into the woods never to be heard from again?"

"It depends."

She snuck a look at him. "On what?"

"On whether either of us are naked when we do it."

She laughed softly, finding the release relaxed her even further. "You have a one-track mind."

"I never said I didn't." His thumbs pressed on the back of her neck and he slowly, deliberately drew them down the length of her spine. She couldn't help a delicious shiver.

"So tell me, Kell, what else is worrying you?"

You, she wanted to say, but didn't dare. To do so would reveal more than she was ready to at this point. "How much do you know about my father?" she asked.

"You mean aside from the fact that he'd like to have my head served up on a platter?"

She caught herself smiling. "Yeah."

"Not much, really. I know he's been on the force for a long time. Why?"

She ignored his question. "Do you know anything about my mother?"

His hands stilled on her back and he didn't say anything for a long moment. After a couple of heartbeats, Kelli regretted asking the question.

She didn't talk to anyone about her mother, not even Bronte. And on the occasions when she'd tried to talk to her father about her, he'd frozen her out—a reaction she still couldn't quite comprehend. Holidays, birthdays and Mother's Day went by without even a passing mention by her father. It was almost as if Loretta Jane Hatfield had never existed, even though Kelli's own existence was proof positive she had.

David cleared his throat. "Should I know something about your mother?" he asked.

She peeked at him over her shoulder. "No. Like you said, things tend to make the rounds at the station."

"Some things," he clarified.

She turned back around and bit thoughtfully on her bottom lip.

"Tell me about her," David said softly, coaxing her to drop her head forward.

Kelli closed her eyes again, envisioning the picture of the woman on her bulletin board at home. But she remembered more than that. She recalled Sunday afternoons making brownies in their Georgetown kitchen, of licking the spoon and getting more of the chocolaty mix on herself than in the pan. She remembered stringing long garlands of cranberries and popcorn, then hanging them on the tree next to handmade ornaments. She recollected cuddling up on her twin bed with her mother on cold nights like these. She'd pull the quilt up to her chin as her mother read her *Heidi* or *Little Women* or *Wuthering Heights*, books her father had thought were too old for her but she had loved just the same. It had made her feel like an adult. Later she'd since figured out her mother had left out some of the racier passages, tailoring the stories for her young ears.

She smiled softly. It had been so long since she'd thought of her mother as more than a lifeless shape under a white sheet. It felt good to remember the loving person she'd been.

"Kelli?" David said softly, his words closer to her ear than she expected. "You aren't falling asleep on me, are you?"

She shook her head. "No. Sorry. I was just remembering my mom."

His fingers shifted from her shoulders to trace soft lines against her scalp. She hummed her approval and dropped her head back.

"She died when I was seven years old."

His hands slowed. "I'm sorry."

"Don't be. You're not the one who did it."

"Does that mean she was—"

"She was murdered."

"Was her killer caught?"

She swallowed. "No." She absently curved her arms around her torso.

"That's got to be tough."

"What's tougher is trying to find leads left dangling for over eighteen years."

He removed his hands altogether. "You're not saying what I think you are."

"What? That I've been working on the case on and off for the past four years? Yes, I guess I am."

She had no idea why she was sharing all of this with him. No one else knew about her covert activities except the detective she'd talked into copying her mother's case files for her—and he'd only agreed because he was the older brother of one of her academy partners. She'd tried to tell her father once. But it was so obvious he wasn't ready to hear the information that she'd stopped just short of blurting it out.

That she was telling David everything now was puzzling at best, disturbing at worst.

She prided herself on her independence. Despite her and her father's closeness over the years, when it came to her mother, she'd always been on her own.

She gave a small shiver.

"Are you cold?"

She shook her head. "No." Truth be told, she was feeling a bit warm. His older apartment was like hers in that it had radiant heat, making it nearly unbearably warm.

She gave a tiny gasp when she felt his fingers edging up under the back of her shirt, touching the flesh there.

"With all you've taken on, no wonder you look like you're about to drop," he said.

Thick tendrils of awareness curled through her belly. "I always said you were a flatterer."

"You know what I mean."

"Yeah, I do." And she did. That he glimpsed just a bit of the pressure she was under was comforting somehow. Almost as comforting as the fingers sliding against her bare back. "You have to promise me, you know, that you won't tell anyone that I'm investigating my mother's case on my own."

"It never crossed my mind. But..." His words trailed off.

"But?"

"But do you think you should really be doing that? I mean, with all you've already got going on, investigating your mother's death on the side...well, isn't it too much?"

"Sometimes. It's just that it's something I have to do. The three years I was in New York I barely opened the files because there wasn't much I could do there."

"So the instant you got back here you started up again."

"Yes."

His fingers edged upward to where the strap of her bra should have been. It was only then that she remembered she wasn't wearing one. And the halting of his hands in the area in question told her he just figured it out, as well.

"Uh, Hatfield? Aren't you missing some...underwear?"

"Missing is a funny word to use, don't you think?" She smiled. "I usually don't wear one this late."

"Uh-huh. I'll have to remember that."

She lightly drove her elbow back, catching him in the ribs.

"Ooof. Hey, I'm just making conversation."

"Uh-huh." It was then Kelli realized just how very close he was. When he'd turned her on the couch, he must have shifted himself, and she was cradled in the vee of his thighs. His chest was mere inches away from her back, leaving just enough room for him to work his magic with his fingertips. His mouth when he spoke to her was close enough to stir the hair over her right ear.

All she had to do was lean back and she'd be ensconced in the warmth of his arms.

She found the prospect very tempting indeed.

DAVID WASN'T SURE exactly when the mood had shifted, but he grew very aware of the charge in the air between him and Kelli. Telltale signs were the way she wriggled her behind backward until she was nearly pressing against his groin, the new shallowness of her breathing, the slight arch in her back as he slid his hands up the silky expanse of skin.

He didn't know a woman could be so soft. He remembered thinking recently that under Kelli's innocent exterior was steel. How wrong he'd been. While she was one of the strongest women he'd ever met, the reasons behind her prickly demeanor and steadfast ambition were as soft as they came.

Her sweet-smelling hair tickled his nose and he fought the desire to close his eyes and groan. He knew without asking that her sharing what she had marked a milestone of sorts in their relationship, even if she refused to admit that they had one. And her talking about her mother made him think of the lack of a mother in his own life.

Up and down, back and forth, he methodically moved his fingers along the now pliable muscles of her back, trying to ignore how damn good she felt.

He hadn't given much thought to his own mother except when he and his brothers and Pops trudged out to her burial site once a year on the anniversary of her death. He supposed it was because he'd never known her. He was two when she'd died. Too young to remember anything. And his brothers and his father hadn't been much good at filling in the gaps. Not that he'd ever asked them to. His not having a mother was just a fact that he'd lived with. An unquestionable reality that was part of his life.

But the way Kelli had smiled when remembering hers made him wonder how things might have been different had his mother lived. What it would have been like to have a woman around the house when he was growing up.

"My mother died when I was very young," he found himself saying.

Kelli looked at him over her shoulder, her eyes curious. "I'm sorry."

He'd said the same thing to her a short while ago. Why was it that you always felt the need to apologize for something you had no control over when someone mentioned the death of a loved one? Maybe it was the need to say something, anything, to let the other person know you cared. And that Kelli cared made his stomach feel oddly weightless.

"Don't be. You couldn't have stopped the cancer any sooner than I could." He raised his hand to her neck, forcing her to face forward again. "It never really bothered me, you know, her not being there. Maybe because I was too young to remember anything. But my brothers and Pops keep telling me that when I was six or so I ran away to a neighboring ranch to live with a family that had both parents intact."

She reached around and caught his wrist, neither squeezing nor pulling. Just holding.

"I don't remember that either, but they say I fought like a bear when they tried to take me back home." He chuckled softly. "I don't know, I sometimes think they're just pulling my leg, getting back at me for pulling the pranks I have. Only they always use the same story."

Kelli's voice dropped to a whisper. "Which means it's probably true."

He smiled. "Yeah. That's what I thought. Then again, knowing my brothers, I wouldn't put it past them to make up something like that."

"Sounds like they're just like you."

David squinted his eyes. "Yeah. I guess they are."

He'd never really thought of the similarities that connected him to his brothers, only the differences. And it made him feel good to realize that they were bonded together in some important way.

Kelli released his hand, then scooted back a little farther, putting her curvy little bottom in direct contact with him. He'd been semierect since the moment he first began massaging her back, but now he pulsed rock hard. His breath caught in his throat. "Um, Kelli, I think you'd better move a little bit in the other direction."

"Oh, I don't know. I think I like it right where I am." Her quiet laugh told him the evil little wench knew exactly what effect she was having on him.

He tunneled his nose through her hair until it was right next to her ear. "Here I am trying to have a serious conversation and all you can think about is sex."

She started to pull away from him, the alarm on her face evident, but he refused her escape, instead tugging his hands out from under her shirt and hauling her until her back was flush against his front. "I'm just kidding, Kell. Hell, I'd be the last one to object if you wanted to get naked right this minute."

"You're intolerable."

"And you're a tease."

"I am not," she said indignantly.

"Uh-huh. And I suppose your pressing that cute little bottom of yours against me was completely innocent."

He caught her devilish smile. "Well...no."

"Just as I thought. Can you shift a little bit. Good." He moved his left leg from where it was bent at the knee and stretched it out on the other side of her. "There."

He curved his arms around her rib cage, then folded his fingers on top of her flat stomach.

"You know, I really should be getting back home," she said quietly.

"You think so, huh?"

"I have to get up early tomorrow and put in another full day."

David rested his chin against the top of her head. "No rest for the weary and all that."

She placed her hands on top of his and he noticed she was getting more comfortable rather than making any real attempt to move.

"Kojak might have something to say about your leaving, don't you think?"

They both looked over at where the pooch was lying on the sports magazines David had kicked out of the hall. A loud snore that was more like a snort made them both laugh.

For long, quiet moments David just stayed there like that, taking comfort in holding Kelli and reveling in her letting him hold her.

She wriggled slightly, reminding him of his aroused state. "Stop it, Hatfield," he murmured as he closed his eyes.

"What? I'm just trying to get more comfortable."

"Uh-huh."

Silence, then, "David?"

"Shhh."

"Don't shush me," she said, though her whisper took the bite out of her words. She quietly cleared her throat. "I just wanted to tell you...I mean, I want to say..."

"What?"

"Thank you."

He tightened his arms around her and pressed his lips against her hair. He wasn't sure what she was thanking him for. Wasn't sure if he wanted to know. All he wanted to do was lie there and hold her. "You're welcome, Kell. You're very, very welcome."

10

KELLI CLOSED the cash register drawer, then gave a brief glance around the shop. It was hard to believe that around this time last night she was dead on her feet. It was four o'clock and, well, she felt refreshed somehow. Happy. Ready to go another shift with no problem.

She supposed a portion of her mind-set might have something to do with waking up next to David this morning. Somewhere during the night he must have taken off her shoes and her jeans and carried her into his bedroom, but damned if she could remember any of it. She'd briefly wondered what else had happened, then realized she would have remembered if she and David had made love. That wasn't something easily forgotten. So she had snuggled further into his arms and dozed off again, taking comfort in Kojak's weight at the foot of the bed.

She'd never spent the entire night with a man before. And to think that sex hadn't even played a role was doubly astonishing.

She'd awakened an hour or so later to find a note on David's pillow telling her he'd gone to work, but that she should stay put for as long as she wanted. He'd also left a bowl of Cocoa Puffs, a small pitcher of milk and cold toast on the nightstand next to the bed, and when she went into the kitchen she'd found a bowl of dog food and water put out for Kojak. She'd been surprised to find he'd even bought the right diet brand.

Who'd have thought hotshot David McCoy could be so thoughtful?

Kelli caught herself smiling, as she had often throughout the day and made an effort to banish it. If she kept mooning after David every spare moment, she wouldn't be able to catch a shoplifter much less a murderer.

She looked around the place. Not a person in sight. Jose was probably tending to the mostly empty booths in the back, while Jeremy was off on one of his errands, his office door closed.

Biting down on her bottom lip, she looked toward the door again, then inched toward the office. A try of the knob proved it was unlocked. Before she had a chance to second-guess herself, she ducked inside, leaving the door open in case Jeremy came back. It would be bad enough to be caught in the office with him there, much less with the door closed behind her.

With one eye on the shop's activity, or lack thereof, she fingered through the papers on his desk. She'd snooped through the room twice before. There was nothing there but normal business stuff: receipts, purchase orders, a payables ledger. She opened the drawers one by one. Nothing out of the ordinary. Not that she had expected to find anything. Despite his unconventional lifestyle, Jeremy was as conventional as they came.

She picked up a couple of receipts. One was from an adult bookstore on the edge of the city, the other from a racy lingerie shop a mile or two down the street. She frowned. Checking out the competition, maybe?

Most likely.

She put the receipts back down, checked out the video recorder in the corner, flipped through his address book to see if he'd added any names, then let herself back out of the office, closing the door after herself.

Well, that had certainly gotten her far, hadn't it?

She stepped back to the relative safety of the counter. Tugging her small notepad from where she had it stashed inside her bra, she jotted down the names of the last two customers.

Thank God for credit cards, was all she had to say. Made her task of keeping track of people that much easier.

"Making your list and checking it twice?"

Kelli froze. Without her even being aware of it, Jeremy had come back and was grinning at her from the end of the counter. She managed a shaky smile in return. "Yeah, I'm one of those dreaded last-minute shoppers. They'll probably have to kick me out of the stores Christmas Eve." She snapped her notepad closed, then tucked it back into her bra. Jeremy watched her, his gaze lingering on her breasts. "How about you?" she asked. "Have all your Christmas shopping done?"

He sighed and leaned against the counter. "Unfortunately, I don't have that many people to buy for."

"Some would say that's fortunate."

"Yeah, but that also means I don't get very many presents either."

"A definite drawback," Kelli agreed, straightening her skirt. "Look, Jeremy, I really want to thank you for reworking my shift so I could get off early this afternoon. I usually don't do these family things, but this year...I thought it was time to make amends, if you know what I mean."

What she was really hoping was that she could talk to her father at the annual station Christmas party. That is, if he showed up. She felt it somehow important she try to smooth things over between them and move onto neutral territory before Christmas dinner at her aunt Beryl's. She could barely choke down Aunt B's cornbread dressing as it was. With her father glaring at her from across the table, she was afraid she'd choke and require the Heimlich performed on her.

"*De nada*, sweet thing. As you can see, business gets light around this time of year anyway. Everybody getting religion and all that." He grinned. "Not to worry, though, the day after the major event, they flock in here all set to party down for New Year's."

She laughed, then drawled wryly, "Gives a whole new meaning to New Year's resolutions, doesn't it?"

She wasn't sure if it was the lights or the way he was looking at her, but somehow Kelli thought he looked older than she initially pegged him to be. Rather than in his mid-forties, she guessed he was closer to sixty, his light hair camouflaging the patches of gray. Either that or he was in need of a new dye job. She'd pretty much figured out that outside of the shop, he didn't seem to have much of a life. He sat in his office most of the time, reviewing product catalogs and spending a lot of time on his computer. A check of his hard drive and Internet files a couple of nights ago had proved he was as clean with his computer as he was in the store.

"So tell me, Kitty Kat," he said slowly, "you any relation to Loretta Jane Hatfield?"

Kelli's stomach did a double flip that seemed to sit at an uncomfortable angle in her belly. She turned toward the cash register and opened it. "She was my mother." She carefully controlled the pitch of her voice. "Did you know her?"

He crossed his arms and sighed. "Naw. I'm a crime buff and was just doing some run-of-the-mill web surfing a few months ago and came up with the articles related to her death, what was it, twenty years ago?"

"Eighteen." She tossed a smile over her shoulder, wondering why she hadn't come across his interest in crime either in his office or his computer. Good thing she hadn't been in town long, or he might have stumbled across some information on her. As luck would have it, she wasn't even mentioned in any of the pieces run on David recently. "What were you doing? Spying on me, Jeremy?"

"No. Just curious. You looked familiar to me somehow and I was curious as to why." He scanned her. "You look just like her, you know."

Her throat threatened to close up.

"From what I can tell from the pictures, I mean. Quite a looker. And so are you."

"Thanks."

"No need for thanks. I should be thanking you for coming to work for me. You've really brightened things up around here."

"Well, thanks for hiring me."

He reached out and picked up a returned box of scented oils a customer claimed irritated her skin. "Well, now that we've established the mutual appreciation society, I'd better let you go. What time did you say that party started?"

Kelli looked at her watch, then gasped. "Five. And it's a quarter to." She closed the cash drawer, then grabbed her coat where she'd stashed it under the closed counter. "I guess I'll see you tomorrow morning." She smiled. "Can you believe it'll be Christmas Eve?"

"At this point in my life I can believe just about anything. Have a good time, ya hear? I expect you to share every juicy detail when you come in tomorrow."

"You got it." Boy, she was going to have to make a note of his interest in crime and pass it on to the task force. Not that she even remotely believed Jeremy a suspect, but anything crime-related was worth mentioning. She was certain there were things about the case the task force leaders knew and weren't sharing.

She began to pass Jeremy, noticing how sad he looked suddenly. Impulsively, she kissed him on the cheek, then pulled back to look at the surprise on his face. "Thanks again, Jeremy. You're a prince among men."

"Ah, I've always fancied myself a royal."

Kelli waggled her fingers at him, then hurried out the door.

DAVID SAUNTERED into the decorated lobby of the station, immediately hit by the sound of Christmas carols being played on a giant boom box on the counter, and cringing at the garland some of the guys had on around their necks. The majority of the festivities were scheduled to take place in the briefing room where the chairs had been folded up and put away, making room for the fifty-some officers who were expected and their spouses for the party.

David usually breezed through the rooms, wishing everyone a Merry Christmas, then moving on to whatever plans he had on tap. This was the first year he'd actually looked forward to the event. Solely because he had no doubt Kelli would be there.

"It's the Casanova Cop!" O'Leary called out from the front desk. "Hey, everyone, hold onto your wives and girlfriends. D.C.'s most eligible bachelor has just entered the building."

David grinned. "Cute, O'L, real cute. But don't you have to be rich or something to make the most eligible list?"

Janesha in records walked by on her way to the briefing room. "Take it from me, honey, money ain't everything." She kissed him loudly on the cheek. "Oh, no. Sugar like that beats money any day."

Those in the lobby burst into laughter along with David as the woman old enough to be his mother made a play at licking her lips then sashayed from the room. "Mmmm, mmmm."

David raised his hands. "I have it on good authority that Jan is prejudiced. Three years ago I threatened to arrest her landlord when he wanted to evict her for having a cat."

"Always were a sucker for the ladies, weren't you, McCoy?" O'Leary called back.

"I don't have to stand here and take this abuse, you know. In fact, I won't. I'm going to the locker room to change. Anyone have any objections?"

There were a couple of colorful responses, then David shook his head and stepped down the hall toward the showers. He was halfway there when Lieutenant Kowalsky stepped from out of one of the offices and blocked his way.

David's smile melted into a grimace. At least this time he hadn't literally run into the man. "Hey, Kow, you officially off the clock yet?" He realized his mistake even before his superior's eyeballs nearly popped out of his head in surprise. "Oh, geez, sir, I'm sorry. I didn't mean any disrespect—"

"Unlike some people that'll go unmentioned, I'm never off the clock, Officer McCoy."

"Of course, sir."

Kowalsky's sudden warm grin nearly knocked him backward. "And it's quite all right to call me Kow, David. That was my nickname in the service. Been awhile since anyone's had the guts to use it, though. Brings back some memories."

David released a long sigh of relief. "For a minute there I was afraid you were going to knock me into the middle of next week."

"For a minute there, I thought I was, too." Kow put his arm across his shoulders. "Come on, I'll walk you to the locker room."

David watched the man he'd declared enemy long ago out of the corner of his eye. If he didn't know better, he'd think Kow was getting sentimental on him. Must be something in the punch. Then again, he doubted the six foot five man ever touched liquor. Or if he did, it would probably take the entire contents of two heavily spiked punch bowls to even begin to intoxicate him.

Kowalsky cleared his throat. "I heard what you did down on V Street this morning, McCoy. Good job. I just want you to know that I'm making a special note of it in my report."

"Sir?"

"The way you pulled in all the kids from the youth center to work the soup kitchen. I hear it was a great success."

David felt the tips of his ears heat. "Oh, that." He cast a wary glance down the hall. "Don't let word get around. I'm having a hard enough time taking the teasing now, sir."

Kow laughed and gave his shoulder a brief squeeze before releasing him. "Don't let 'em bust your balls, McCoy. You know what you're doing. That's all that matters."

"How about you, sir? You ever play sports?"

"Sports?"

David reveled in his ability to catch his superior off guard. "Yeah, you know. Basketball? Football?"

"I used to be pretty damn good in the boxing ring."

David tried to imagine climbing into a ring and facing him. The image would probably give him nightmares for days. "We could probably use someone with your experience down at the center. You know, if you have the time and all."

Kow's smile widened into a grin. "I'll give it some thought, boy. I'll give it some thought." His gazed flicked over him as if reassessing an earlier opinion. "Now go on, get changed and get back out here and join the party."

The lieutenant did a military style turnabout then marched back down the hall, leaving David staring after him completely dumbfounded.

For the second time in the past half hour, David found himself shaking his head. What else could possibly happen today? First he'd awakened to find Kelli's sweet little body snuggled against him in his own bed, her dog whining at him from where he had his head resting against his feet. Now this.

He didn't know what it was, but he mentally braced himself for a fall. If there was one thing he'd learned early on, it was that with every good eventually came bad.

He caught sight of someone sitting across from his locker. Only it usually took the bad a little time to catch up.

"Hey, Pops," he called out, noticing the wariness laced through his voice.

Ever since he'd learned exactly who Kelli's father was he'd been avoiding Manchester and his father, not looking forward to having a conversation that was sure to get ugly. Too late, he realized that Marc must have spilled the beans.

Damn. It would have been nice to have a few more minutes to glow following Kow's unheard of praise. By the look on his father's face as he got up from the wood bench, it was going to be all downhill from there.

"Hey, yourself." He was still in uniform, still every bit the young cop David had a picture of on the wall at his apartment. He'd never gotten thicker around the middle. If anything, he looked in better shape now than he ever had. Of course, part of the reason for that might be his recent relationship with Melanie's mom, Wilhemenia.

He picked up his step, tossing his cap onto the top shelf of the locker, then hanging his coat. "Got something on your mind, Pops?"

"Yeah, actually I do."

David grimaced. "Figured it had to be something. You know, to bring you downtown and all."

"Yeah."

David glanced at him, curious as to why the old man hadn't gotten to the point yet. No one could say that Sean McCoy was at a loss for words when it came to something important to him. Lord knew he and his brothers had taken their share of tongue-lashings that could rival the world's best over the years. He turned back to his locker and took out his jeans and a green and red sweater that one of the women he had dated a couple years back had given him. It was hideous, but it fit the occasion. He held it up, thought of Kelli, and fought the urge to toss it into the garbage. He would have had he something else to wear.

"Can it wait until I catch a quick shower?"

Sean nodded, but his gaze was concentrated on his shoes. "I suppose."

It made him uncomfortable to see his father at a loss. "Okay. See you in a couple."

He stepped off to the showers, wondering exactly what his father had to say. And exactly when he'd get around to saying it.

KELLI STOOD sipping on the bitter punch, idly wondering how many guys had spiked it and just how potent the tepid liquid was. Someone should have a Breathalyzer waiting outside the station along with a row of taxis if the quick evaporation level of the bowl was anything to go by. Wrinkling her nose, she stepped to the soft drink table, tossed the contents of her plastic cup into the garbage then filled it with clear soda.

She turned and surveyed the room over the rim. She had hoped her father would be hanging around somewhere, but she'd been there for ten minutes and had yet to spot him. Given her lateness, she'd barely had time to stop off at the apartment and change. Having spent all day tottering on stiletto heels and confined in tight clothes she'd opted for a simple pair of dark green slacks with loafers and a cream colored blouse. While she wasn't as dressed up as some of the women there, at least she wasn't wearing anything that was blinking, flashing, or otherwise capturing attention. Right now she preferred just to blend into the background.

As she scanned the room again, she realized her father wasn't the only one she was looking for. Somewhere David McCoy was probably wowing his co-workers with stories of his latest escapades. She had heard what he'd done at the soup kitchen already. Twice.

How in the hell was she supposed to guard her heart against a hotshot cop who could hold her all night without making a move, fix her breakfast and help neighborhood kids and the homeless? She picked up an overiced Christmas cookie and crunched off a bite. She'd initially been appalled by the magazine piece. Casanova Cop, indeed. But the more she thought about it, the more she sincerely believed that David McCoy deserved the better part of the attention he was getting.

Of course, she'd never tell *him* that. The guy already had an ego the size of the Capitol building.

Besides, she didn't think she needed to tell him anything. What he did, he did because he enjoyed doing it, not because he got off on the publicity. If anything, he seemed somewhat embarrassed by the attention. At least when you looked past the grin and paid attention to his ears, which had a tendency to redden when he was embarrassed—yet another endearing detail she had come to learn about him.

Of course if it were up to Kojak, who she'd had to drag from David's apartment that morning, she'd be marrying the guy next week.

She nearly choked on the dry cookie. Turning away from the group next to her, she coughed her way through it, then took a long sip of soda.

Where had *that* thought come from?

"Wrong pipe?"

She swiveled around to find none other than her father standing next to her, looking everywhere but at her. Had he said anything else she might have thought he'd spoken to someone else.

"Yeah. Cookies are, um, a little dry." She gave another glance around, this time furtively. If David *was* around somewhere, she hoped he didn't choose now to pop up. She'd asked her father to come to the party before she'd spent last night with David and hadn't exactly expected to be on speaking terms with the Casanova Cop tonight, much less... What terms *were* they on?

Her father nodded in a stiff way that made her want to groan. Either that or whack him in the arm until he stopped being such a mule.

"Glad you could make it," she said quietly.

He finally looked at her. "Glad you invited me. Even if it was via my answering service."

She grimaced. "Yeah, well, I'd have done it directly if you'd have returned any of my phone calls." She bit down hard on her tongue. This line of conversation wasn't going to get them anywhere. "Sorry," she said quietly.

His eyes softened briefly. "Me, too."

The tension in her shoulders melted away so quickly she nearly slouched in relief. "If that was an apology, then I accept."

His gaze flicked over her smiling face. "I don't want you to get me wrong, Kelli Marie. I am apologizing, but not for what you think I am."

She considered him. "I'm not sure I get you. What *are* you apologizing for, then?"

"For not returning your calls. No matter what happens, it's important to remember that...well, you know."

You and me against the world, kid. It's just you and me against the world.

How was she supposed to argue with that?

She looked away, covertly blinking back tears. He hated it when she cried. She'd learned that very young. Then again, maybe it was time she stopped hiding things from him. She purposefully tipped her chin up, letting him see the tears in her eyes.

He stubbornly looked away.

She took a long sip of her soda then cleared her throat, silent until she'd regained control over her emotions. "Just so I'm straight on this, what you're not apologizing for is everything else."

That drew his gaze back.

"You're still against my working on the task force," she clarified.

He sighed. "Yes."

"You still want to see David McCoy banished from the face of the earth."

His jaw tightened. "Along with that low-down, no-good father of his."

"And you don't think there was anything wrong with your calling me 'girl.'"

He looked suddenly exasperated. "I've called you 'girl' for years, Kelli. Why does it bother you now?"

"Because you said it differently, that's why."

"What?"

"You know what I mean. And if you don't, you need to figure it out." She held her hand up. "Okay, I'll indulge you. Do
you want an example of what I mean?"

His eyes narrowed. "It looks like you're going to give it to
me whether I want you to or not."

She ignored that. "Repeat after me. 'I only want the best for
you, girl.' Then say it again substituting the word 'honey.'"

He didn't utter a word.

"Dad—"

"Okay, okay." Lowering his voice, he repeated the sentence.

"See how the two words 'girl' and 'honey' are interchange-
able? Good. Now repeat this one. 'You don't know what you're
talking about, girl.' And do the same thing with the word
'honey.'"

He didn't do it.

"You can't, can you? Because the meaning isn't the same."

He released a long-suffering sigh. "God, I've raised a mon-
ster."

She cracked a smile. "No, Dad, you didn't. You raised a person who expects respect. Even from you."

An unfamiliar something shone from his eyes. For a moment
she thought it was the very respect she'd been after.

"Now, about the other issue…"

He quickly held up a hand. "Can it hold? I'm really not up to
discussing that now…honey."

She laughed. "Sure. We can discuss it later. Just so long as
we agree to discuss it."

"Good."

"Great."

She hooked her arm through his, giving it a squeeze. Lowering her voice, she said, "Does this mean you're going to go
back to calling me every hour on the hour?"

He gave her a warning glance.

"Good. I've missed those calls."

BACK IN THE locker room, David sat forward on the bench, trying to absorb everything his father had just entrusted to him. Twenty minutes of detail-loaded monologue that left his head swimming. He frowned at his father where he sat next to him. "That's what all this is about? This whole feud thing between you and Garth Hatfield? Because he used to date Mom?"

Sean's face grew unbelievably red. "He didn't just used to date her. He tried to steal her from me."

"While you two were partners."

"Yeah."

David scratched his head, then ran his fingers through his still damp hair. "I don't get it. You and Mom got married despite what you think Hatfield did, right? So why still the bad blood?"

"Because Garth tried—"

"Yeah, yeah, I got it the first time, Pops. Because Garth tried to steal her from you." He leaned back and studied the ceiling. "Let's see, here it is thirty-something years—"

"Thirty-eight."

"Okay, thirty-eight years and five kids later in your case, and a marriage and another kid in his, and you're still holding this grudge." He threw up his hands in exasperation. "Hey, makes perfect sense to me."

"I knew you'd understand once I explained everything."

David grimaced. "That was said tongue-in-cheek, Pops. It doesn't make *any* sense, especially considering how close it looks like you two might have been."

"We were never close," he said vehemently.

"Yeah, right. That's why you're still upset about all of this."

Sean looked at him, a very familiar shadow of sadness, of grief, coloring his eyes. "You just don't understand."

David sat forward again. "I want to, Pops. I really do." He

sighed. "Look, maybe I...we both need some time to think this through. It was dumb of me to think a thirty-something—"

"Thirty-eight."

"Yeah. It was stupid of me to think I could undo in a half hour conversation what has been years in the making." He patted his father on the back. "Let's say we go out and have a drink, huh? I don't know about you, but after all this I sure could use one."

Sean smiled for the first time since David spotted him in the locker room. "So could I."

KELLI LAUGHED at a particularly ribald joke one of her fellow officers had just shared with her and her father, feeling completely at ease for the first time in far too long. She and her father were not only talking again, they were talking at the station, a place she had never dared talk about to her father before, simply because he wanted to forget where she worked. That he was here, that he was treating her like a work equal was saying a lot.

Then there was David. She and he...well, they were doing *something* again, and even if she didn't know exactly what that meant, that felt good, too.

"Merry Christmas, Chief Hatfield."

Kelli nearly dropped her soda at the sound of the familiar voice. In one split second it appeared everything was going to change.

She turned toward where David was addressing her father, his hand outstretched, a congenial smile on his face. "I don't know if you recall, but we have met before, however unofficially. I want to say what a pleasure it is to see you again."

Oh, God.

Kelli didn't know quite what to do. She was caught between wanting to launch herself at David, get him away from the immediate area ASAP and grabbing her father to keep him from doing anything rash. It didn't surprise her that her father completely ignored David's hand. It didn't shock her that the entire room had just fallen completely silent. What did amaze her was that cool, calm and in control Garth Hatfield pulled back his arm as if in slow motion, then hauled off and punched David right in the jaw.

11

IN THE MIDDLE of the briefing room floor, David propped himself up on his elbows, staring at the huge man who had just clocked him. Wow. Garth Hatfield might be an old guy, but he still packed a helluva wallop. Maybe he'd have to rethink his entire approach to this whole Hatfield and McCoy feud, because there was obviously more bad blood here than he'd realized.

"Why you..." Pops emerged from the crowd that had gathered, zooming in on his archenemy like a gang member out for blood. A unified gasp went up as Kelli stepped in front of her father and David scrambled to his feet to stop his father. As much as he'd like to see Pops get some payback, this thing had already gone far enough already. And two days before Christmas even.

David noticed several of his closer coworkers, including Kow, step up ready to provide reinforcements.

Pops struggled against him. "Let me at 'im, David. Nobody sucker punches a son of mine and lives to tell the story."

Garth strained against Kelli's blocking arm. David looked down to where she had her leg ready to trip him up should he try to go any further. "No son of yours touches my little girl without paying the price."

David slanted a glance at Kow who raised a brow and looked between him and Kelli. Damn. So much for keeping that little detail a secret.

Sean McCoy looked ready to pop his lid. He jabbed a finger

in Garth's direction. "You've been angling for this for a long time, Hatfield. And I'm only too happy to give it to you."

"*I've* been angling for this? What about you, McCoy? I wouldn't be surprised if you put your son up to this just to get back at me."

"Yeah, well, maybe I did. Lord knows it would serve you right, you pigheaded, self-absorbed, sorry excuse for a chief."

This time it was Kelli's brows that rose. David groaned. "That's enough, Pops. This isn't the time or the place for this." He stumbled a couple of steps backward, his father's strength and determination proving more of a match for him than he thought possible. "Now tell the good man here that you didn't put me up to anything."

Sean finally stopped struggling and stepped back. He pulled the ends of his uniform jacket down to straighten it. "I'll do no such thing."

"Now, Pops—"

"Let the man speak, boy," Hatfield ordered.

David grimaced as Kelli released her father and stood stiffly between the two men. "I think there's been enough talking done around here already. All those who agree with me, say 'aye,'" she called out.

A series of in sync "ayes" echoed through the suddenly quiet room, though David made out a couple wanting to see a fight.

Kelli grimaced. "Okay, I think it's time for you to go, Daddy."

Garth Hatfield first appeared ready to plow right through his own daughter, then dropped his gaze, his face flushing an even deeper shade of red. "I don't see why I have to go first," he mumbled under his breath, much like a five-year-old who'd just been involved in his first scuffle.

"You have to go first because I invited you here and you've just embarrassed me beyond belief so I am officially uninviting you." She lifted her hand and pointed at the door as if addressing that sulky five-year-old. "Go. Now."

Garth appeared ready to do exactly as she requested. With that done Kelli turned toward David and his father. David blinked at her, impressed, proud, and disgustingly turned on. "If you wish to press charges, Officer McCoy, I'd be more than happy to take the report."

"Report!" Garth shouted.

Without even turning, Kelli stomped her foot and pointed to the door.

David eyed his father. "Pops? Is it safe for me to let you go now?"

Sean McCoy stared after his adversary as he stormed from the room.

"It would be nice if you answered me, like, sometime today," David prompted.

As soon as Garth was gone, Sean seemed to deflate. He dragged in a deep breath then exhaled gustily. For the first time, it seemed, he looked at Kelli. And to David's disbelief, he smiled, however shyly. "I don't think my son will press charges Officer Hatfield. If it's all the same to you, this is something your father and I have to work out outside official channels."

"I think you both need to have your heads examined," David said under his breath, then grinned at Kelli's glare.

He made a production out of rubbing his throbbing jaw. "What?" he asked innocently enough.

Kow stepped up and faced the crowd. "Okay, folks, the fun's all over now. Go back about your business," he said. "And Merry Christmas."

David felt the most absurd need to laugh. Not a brief chuckle, but a side-clutching, hysterical kind of laugh that would leave him back on the floor, rolling to catch his breath.

"Come on, Pops," he said, putting his arm over Sean's shoulders. "I think that's our cue to get you out of here, too."

"McCoy!" Kow barked. "I think your father is capable of seeing himself home. You, Hatfield and I have some unfinished business."

TWO DAYS LATER, Kelli let herself into her apartment, closed the door, then stripped out of her shoes, stockings and dress as she made her way to her bedroom. Overjoyed that his daylong sentence to solitary confinement was at its end, Kojak followed her around, barking, bounding and sniffing after each item as she dropped it to the floor.

"Merry Christmas, Jack," she murmured, giving him a playful wrestle. "But if it's all the same to you, I'd prefer to stick with 'bah, humbug.'"

The two days since the humiliating incident at the stationhouse Christmas party felt like two weeks. Her head ached, her muscles twitched and she basically just wished the whole blasted holiday season were over so she would stop having to be so nice to everyone when she felt like growling.

First there had been the lecture on proper conduct by Kow that she and David had sat through in his office, away from the party crowd. He'd given it to them good, getting them to spill that they'd not only known each other before they were paired together, but that they'd been, um, somewhat intimately involved. Given Kelli's task force assignment, he'd said he'd let the situation slide for now, but that they had better be on their best behavior at the station for the next six months at least. So thorough had the lieutenant stripped a piece off of them that David had whispered that he didn't think it was a good idea if they left together, so they hadn't. And he hadn't shown up later at her place, either, as she'd hoped he would.

Speaking of the task force, everyone was fearful that the D.C. Executioner had plans to play the Grinch—his own little gruesome Christmas gift to the citizens of D.C.—so they had instructed her and the other female officers working undercover at area adult bookstores to request double shifts, and the survellience teams were put on extra alert. So yesterday, on Christmas Eve, she'd worked from 9:00 a.m. until 7:00 p.m., when Jeremy had shooed her home. That had been fine with her. Despite the fears she shared with the task force commander, she'd been bushed. She'd dragged herself home and straight to bed and hadn't even woken up again until after nine this morning. That meant she'd been late getting to her aunt's in Baltimore. And she hadn't had a chance to talk to either her father or David since the socking-in-the-jaw incident.

She sank down onto her bed and worked all the pins from her hair, sighing in relief. Sitting across from her sour-faced father all day had been a lesson in patience. No matter where she went, there he was, smack-dab across from her. Gift giving, across from her. Dinner, across from her. In the kitchen helping to clean up…the stylish island where the sink was located allowed him to sit across from her even then.

It would have been okay had he had something nice to say. But every time he'd opened his mouth some kind of underhanded jab was sent flying her way. From "I can't believe you'd side with that pissant over me," to "the way you're acting, you're no daughter of mine." Even her aunt had reached the bottom of her infinite well of patience and whacked him in the arm as they were leaving.

Yes, this was certainly one Christmas for the picture albums. There she would be rolling her eyes toward the ceiling with her father hovering somewhere on the fringes glowering at her.

Kojak whined and thrust his cold, slimy nose in the valley between her toes and the ball of her foot. She jerked back and laughed. "Oh, Kojak, you certainly know how to put things back into perspective, don't you, boy. Thank God I always have you." She rubbed him behind the ears, enjoying his soft murmurs of satisfaction. "Easy to please, you are. I can leave you alone all day and you'll still rush to the door, happy to see me. You couldn't give a hoot who I spent the time away with, or whether or not I worked at a brewery or on the force. Just so long as I throw a treat your way every now and again, you're putty in my hands."

She plopped back on the mattress and patted the comforter beside her. Kojak immediately jumped up, laying his head against her belly. She closed her eyes and patted him, wondering if this was how she was destined to lead her life. An old maid with a dedicated dog instead of a house full of cats.

Unbidden, an image of David McCoy unfurled in her mind, as handsome as all get out and larger than life. She smiled. She couldn't help herself. Whenever she thought of him hitting the floor and blinking at her father in undisguised shock, she felt like laughing. He'd been so damn cute. And so magnanimous. He'd taken the knock and gotten right back up. If his father hadn't lunged for hers, she wouldn't have been surprised if David had turned the other cheek then offered up his hand to her father again.

She had no idea what he had on tap for today. She knew he was scheduled to work last night, something about a favor for a friend. But he'd likely spent today at his family's.

She groaned and rubbed her nose. "You probably made a helluva first impression on Sean McCoy, Kell."

She wondered if the day had been as torturous for David as it had been for her. But she doubted it. She still couldn't believe Sean hadn't wanted his son to press charges. If the roles had been reversed, her father would have stopped at nothing to see that both McCoys were locked up well into the new year.

If she knew more about what had happened so many years ago, maybe she could understand why these two men wanted to dance around a room like it was a boxing ring saying "put up your dukes, put up your dukes." But she knew no more now than she had a few days ago when her father first voiced his disapproval of David simply because of his relationship to a man he didn't like.

The sound of someone knocking at the front door snagged her attention. Kojak lifted his head and gave an experimental sniff. "What do you say, Jackie boy? Do we see if there's any Christmas spirit to be had and open it, or just lie here and pretend this is just like every other day and ignore it?"

Another sniff, then Kojak barked and ran toward the door. Kelli sighed. "I guess that means we open it."

Clad in only her black slip, she padded through the living room then peeked through her peephole.

Nothing.

Frowning, she leaned back, nearly tripping over Kojak. She looked down and watched a treat roll from under the door and stop right in front of the expectant pooch. Shaking her head, Kelli looked through the peephole again. Sure enough, David unfolded himself and grinned at her through the hole.

She unlocked the door, then opened it. "I hope he's not the only one you brought a treat for," she said, leaning against the jamb.

He held up his hands. "Guess you're going to have to settle for the package in front of you."

She grabbed his shirtfront and pulled him into the apartment. "You'll do."

He chuckled. "Wait a second. I was just joking."

She blinked at him as he ducked back into the hall and produced a red foil-wrapped package about the size of a shoebox.

"Oh, David, why did you have to go and do that? I didn't even think to buy you—"

He leaned forward and stole the words from her mouth with a searing kiss. "Don't worry, darlin'. This gift is for both of us."

"Ooo, chocolate?"

His gaze burned a trail down her exposed skin, reminding her of what she had on, which was not much. "No, but it's something almost as good." He pushed the door shut with his foot and came inside, shrugging out of his coat. "Though I'm more interested in exploring what's in your nicely dressed package."

She crossed her arms, deciding she was decently covered despite the indecent expression on his face. "I just got home."

"I know. I've been waiting outside for the past half hour."

"I'm impressed."

"Don't be. I used the time to catch a much-needed catnap." She headed toward the kitchen. "Can I get you something?"

"You got any nog?"

"As in eggnog?"

He grinned. "Yeah."

"No."

"Okay, a beer will do then."

"Well, since you didn't bring any, how do you feel about homemade hot chocolate?"

"Homemade? This, I've got to see."

She padded into the kitchen, unsurprised when he followed her. "So how did it go last night?" she asked.

"On the streets of D.C. on Christmas Eve? Let's just say a lot of creatures were stirring. Somehow I never get used to putting a Santa Claus behind bars."

She clucked her tongue. "Just think of all the kids that didn't get their presents this morning."

"I was more concerned with getting the drunk and disorderly Santa off the street before he completely ruined his reputation."

She laughed, then smacked his hand away from the gourmet chocolate bar she'd taken from the cupboard. "There won't be enough for the hot chocolate."

"Looks like there's plenty there to me."

She popped a square into her own mouth. "Yeah, but that's for the cook."

He leaned forward. "You've got," he kissed the corner of her mouth, "a little bit," he drew his tongue the length of her lower lip, "right here." He kissed her fully, causing Kelli's knees to go as soft as the marshmallows on the counter. "Mmm. It tastes better on you."

She worked her fingers between their mouths then slid a chocolate square between his lips. "Yeah, and if you don't stop, I'm going to burn the milk and ruin my best pan."

He chuckled and munched on the treat. "Okay, I'll wait."

She narrowed her gaze playfully. "Just what do you have planned, Officer McCoy?"

He shrugged. "Not much."

He wandered out of the kitchen, Kojak following on his heels. Moments later the strains of Bing Crosby Christmas carols filled the interior of the apartment. She grimaced, remembering the frightful day spent at her aunt's where they'd been playing the same music. Then she realized he'd changed the channel, scanning for something else. Judging the milk warm enough, she dropped the chocolate squares in one at a time, finishing as a bass thrumming, bluesy song reached her ears. It took her a minute to recognize the same Christmas carol played in a completely different way. A tiny thrill shimmied down her spine. Trust David to somehow make even Christmas Day sexy.

She smiled, then dipped her finger into the pan. She started to pop it into her mouth when David curled his fingers around her wrist and slid it into his mouth instead. "Mmm. This just might be worth waiting for," he said, drawing her finger into the depths of his mouth again.

Kelli watched his decadent lips curve around her knuckle. She was mesmerized, not just by the action itself, but by the man.

As she licked her own suddenly scorched lips, she wondered at everything that went into making one certain David McCoy. She just wasn't the type to fall into such an intimate relationship. It had taken her and Jed six weeks before they made it to bed the first time, then the second had come a month after that. She wasn't exactly sure why she was overprotective when it came to matters of intimacy. It could be Bronte's poor track record. Or it could be that somehow the lack of closure in her own mother's death made her overly wary of opening her heart to anyone. But she realized that with David, all her defenses melted on command. More specifically *his* command.

He dragged his mouth from her finger. "I, um, think something's burning."

She swallowed hard. "Yeah, me."

Her hands trembling, she removed the pan from the heat then poured the contents into two extra large mugs. Then came a handful of tiny marshmallows, whipped cream, and chocolate shavings.

She picked up both mugs.

"What, no cherries?" David asked.

"This is hot chocolate, not an ice-cream sundae." She couldn't help smiling. "But if you want, there's a jar in the cupboard next to the fridge."

He followed her into the living room, palming the extra large jar of maraschinos. "I knew you were my kind of gal."

Kelli laughed softly. "They, um, were on sale."

"Uh-huh."

He plopped down on the oversize couch next to her after she had placed the overflowing mugs down on the table. She tucked her legs under her, then picked up her mug, motioning for him to do the same. She noticed with interest that he left the cherries untouched. Once he was facing her, mug raised, she gently touched hers against his and said, "Here's to Christmas being over this year."

David's blue eyes twinkled. "Here's to the real festivities beginning."

She sipped hers and he did the same, licking the cream from his lips with heavenly abandon. "Now that's what I call hot chocolate."

Kojak whined at her feet. Kelli curved the fingers of her other hand around her mug then reached down to pat him. "What is it, K? Feeling a little left out?" She glanced toward

David. "Watch this." She cleared her throat, then removed her hand. "Okay, you can open your gift now."

She had barely finished her sentence when Kojak charged the tree in the corner at full speed, his skid pushing in the tree skirt. He nosed through the few gifts left there, then came up with his. Growling, he locked his meaty jaws around it, then whipped it back and forth, sending the loose wrapping flying. In no time at all he was stretched across the floor chomping down on his own pooch chocolate chew.

Kelli smiled at David who was chuckling. "Quite a kid you've got there, Hatfield."

"Yeah, I'm pretty proud." Despite her guilt at not having bought him anything, her gaze kept trailing to the present sitting on the edge of the coffee table nearer to him. "So are you planning on letting me open that or not?"

"It's not that type of gift."

"And what type is that?"

"The kind you unwrap and display on your mantel for all to see."

"Ah, so it's something you wear?"

"Well, kind of."

She squinted at him. "Either it is or it isn't."

"Okay, then, it isn't."

She stretched her legs out, tucking her feet under his muscular thigh. "I think that deserves some explanation."

He followed the curve of her leg up from heel to knee to the hem of her black slip. "Let's just say it's the kind of gift better experienced."

Kelli closed her eyes and groaned. "Considering where I'm assigned, I'd suggest you not leave things to my imagination."

He grinned. "Then I won't. Go take a shower."

She wrinkled her nose. "Huh?"

"I said go take a shower." He dropped a kiss to her bare knee, then swirled his tongue along her skin and kissed her again. "Not that you need one, mind you. I just need to buy some set-up time."

"Set-up time—"

He slid his hand up the inside of her leg until his fingertips were mere millimeters away from her panties. "Has anyone ever told you that you ask too many questions?"

"Yeah," she whispered. "You."

He swept her feet down until they were resting on the rug. "Uh-uh. No matter how incredibly sexy you are, you are not going to sidetrack me. Now go on. I need at least fifteen minutes."

She got up and slowly began making her way toward the bathroom. "Fifteen minutes, huh?"

"Yep."

"Should I wash my hair?"

"Nope."

"Then I can be done in five."

He eyed her over the rim of his mug of hot chocolate. "Ten."

"Deal."

She rushed to the bathroom and closed the door. She hadn't felt this giddy since...well, since she couldn't remember when. Maybe when she was about five and still believed in Santa Claus. She stripped down and climbed into the shower, only to reach out a minute later dripping wet to fumble for the fragranced soaps Bronte had given her for her birthday that she'd used only for decoration until now.

She was quickly blotting herself dry in a cloud of steam when a knock sounded at the door. It opened a crack and David's hand appeared through it. "Here. Put this on."

She took the scrap of black silk and turned it one way then the next. "Uh, David, I don't think this is going to cover me."

His chuckle reminded her that he had yet to close the door. "I hope not. It's a blindfold."

"Oh." Then it hit her. "A blindfold. David, I don't—"

"Just put it on, Hatfield. Oh, and as sexy as the little slip is, leave it, okay?"

A delicious shiver of anticipation slithered down her back. What exactly did he have planned?

"Is it on yet?"

She hurriedly tucked the towel, and nothing but the towel, around herself, then smiled. "No."

"Well, get hopping already, Hatfield. Sheesh."

She carefully tied the blindfold around her head, leaving just a slit to look out of. "Okay."

She heard the door open completely, then saw his bare feet as he entered the room, though the hem of his jeans told her he was at least still partially dressed. "Nice try," he said. "Turn around."

She played at a groan as he fastened the blindfold more securely. No matter how hard she tried, she couldn't make out a thing through the dark fabric.

"There." He grasped her shoulders and swiveled her back around. "God, you smell good."

Kelli fought the need to put her hands out in front of her as he led her back out into the living room. It was so odd to move through her apartment, knowing it was her apartment, but still not knowing exactly where everything was with her eyes closed. She felt something warm on the back of her leg, then that same something swept up and cupped her bottom. She gasped, realizing it was David's hand.

His chuckle sounded above her ear. "Sorry. I couldn't resist."

"Just don't do it again," she whispered. "I thought it was Kojak for crying out loud."

"K's in the kitchen for the duration."

"Oh."

Funny how everything smelled differently with the blindfold on. Scents she normally didn't pay any attention to now stood out in stark relief. She picked up the tang of lemon furniture polish. The pine of the small tree. She swore she could even make out the chocolate in the mugs probably still on the coffee table.

"Hold up," he told her.

She stopped, then put her foot out, feeling that same coffee table. Only it wasn't where it was supposed to be. He'd obviously moved it.

"This way," he said, gently gripping her elbow.

The scent of something strong and pungent reached her nose and she wrinkled it. "What's that?"

"What's what?"

"That smell."

He tugged on the bottom of her towel. She gasped and grabbed the top. "You'll find out soon enough." He maneuvered her so she was facing him. "Now, feel the cushion behind you? I want you to sit down on it."

What was her sofa cushion doing on the floor? And what was it covered with? She slowly did as he asked, trying to keep the towel wrapped around her.

"Oh, and you won't be needing that."

With a quick swoosh, he took the towel from around her.

Kelli blindly groped for it, feeling more than naked. She felt suddenly very, very vulnerable. She reached for the blindfold.

"Uh-uh," David caught her hands, coming to sit beside her. "You're beautiful, Kell. Just trust me, will you?"

"Trust you? First you blindfold me like some—"

His mouth, sizzling and wet, trapped the rest of her words in her mouth. She tried to protest, then his tongue flicked out, played along her lips, then plunged into the depths of her mouth. She groaned and collapsed, boneless and towel-less, against him.

After long moments, he dragged his mouth from hers, his breathing ragged. "If we keep on like that, I'll never see this through."

"See what through?" she whispered. "David, let me take off—"

"Here," he said, ignoring her and pressing her back on the cushion. Only she realized it wasn't just one cushion, but probably every cushion and pillow in the apartment, covered by some sort of silky fabric. She tried to peek out from under the blindfold but it was still very much in place.

"You have the most incredible mouth," David murmured, then kissed the side of it. Kelli turned her head to meet him straight on, then felt his breath on the other side. Frustrated, she trapped his head between her hands and brought him down for a deep, soul-searching kiss.

He chuckled softly as he drew back. "I knew I should have tied your hands."

She started to lift herself up. "David, I'm not sure I like—"

"Shhh." Then his mouth was on her breast. She gasped as he swirled his tongue around the instantly hard tip then pulled it deep into his mouth, seeming to manipulate cords that stretched down to between her legs. She lay against the cushions and arched her back. He drew away, then ran his hands the length of her arms, lifting them above her head. "Now that's more like it. Stay just...like that."

His weight shifted away from her. There was that smell again. Kelli curled her hands into the sleek material above her head.

"Now this may be a little cold," he murmured.

"What may—" She drew in a ragged breath as something brushed against her other breast. A tiny little flick of something...wet. Something cold and wet. Definitely not his mouth. Her nipple instantly responded, growing hard and achy even as the first flick was followed by another. Then another. Then the flicks turned into curved swirls.

Kelli clutched the fabric above her head for dear life, feeling the growing heat between her legs compensate for the cold of the substance. David moved to the other breast, doing the same there, not satisfied until she was trying to force a more solid contact. Then he shifted and moved in ever-widening circles until her entire chest was covered with the cold matter. Kelli thought she would go insane with pleasure. She went from being completely relaxed to wondrously excited as he painted her—somewhere in the thick cloud of desire that fogged up her mind she had realized that's what he was doing.

He drew a slow, cold, languid trail down the middle of her stomach. She sucked in air as he circled her navel, then filled it with the cold, wet substance.

"What...what is that?" she whispered.

Then that something wet flicked against her most sensitive part and she gasped.

David's mouth was against her ear. "No questions."

An almost unbearable ache filled her belly, threatening to consume her with need. She quickly nodded. "Okay...okay. No questions."

Another flick and she nearly climaxed right then and there.

"No words either."

Kelli pressed her lips tightly together, drawing quick, rapid breaths in from her nose until her need for air demanded she open her mouth.

Again, he was on her stomach, drawing long, languorous lines down to her hips. The mere movement alone seemed to concentrate all her thoughts there, all her heat, until she was afraid she would cry out from the exquisite pleasure of it all.

He drew the wetness down the inside of one thigh, then up the other, then down again, until her legs were covered. The wanton that apparently dwelled deep within her emerged, and she inched her legs open.

"Good...girl." David's voice was husky and his own breathing sounded nearly as irregular as hers.

Questions filled Kelli's mind, but she was rendered completely speechless, trapped as she was in her black world of pure, sensual sensation. Of smell, of touch, of sound.

Earlier, he'd asked her to trust him. And in that telling moment, she realized she did. Completely. Utterly. Irreversibly. With every flick of his brush, he did away with another of the sexual walls she'd spent so much of her adult life erecting. With each skillful touch, he prepared her for an ecstasy she could only wonder at. She was his to do with what he pleased and she had faith that he would do only that which would bring her joy.

The brush swiped across the bud nestled between her thighs again. She cried out, instantly climaxing. Pleasure rippled along her taut muscles, surprising her with their intensity as she clasped her thighs together. Long moments later, she sank back against the cushions as the golden sensations subsided, the sound of her panting filling her ears.

David's voice was low and gravelly as he tsked at her. "Now look what you've gone and done. You've, um, gotten my...work all wet. I'll just have to clean up and start all over again."

She knew instantly that the something touching her now was David's mouth lapping up the edible paint. Her back came up off the pillows. His tongue burrowed through her damp curls. He followed the shallow crevice of throbbing flesh, each touch of his tongue like the flick of flames. Then his fingers were spreading her and he swirled his tongue around her swollen core. She whimpered uncontrollably, breathlessly begging him to come to her, to end the exquisite torture. Then he took a more intense taste, pulling her deep into his mouth. Another climax threatened to follow quickly after the last. She went rigid in preparation when all too abruptly, his heat was gone.

Kelli's panting sounded foreign to her own ears as she sank back, utterly boneless against the makeshift bed.

"You even taste like a peach," David said so softly she nearly didn't hear him. He ran his finger along the length of her. "There. All clean."

She blindly reached out, desperate to feel him inside her, filling her, needing to share her pleasure with him. But he hovered just beyond reach.

"Shhh," he murmured. Something rested against her lower lip. She opened her mouth and she immediately recognized the smooth skin and sharp tang of a cherry. She chewed slowly, then turned into David's kiss.

"I'll be there soon enough, Kell," he whispered. "Just relax." The brush again flicked against the crux of her heat. She shuddered from the contrast between hot and cold.

"Please," she whimpered, her legs thrashing wildly even as he tried to hold them in place.

"Almost done," he whispered, giving another feather-light flick. "There."

For long moments Kelli lay there, hearing nothing but the sound of her own breathing. In and out. In and out. Where was he? She hadn't heard him leave. And he wasn't touching her anymore. Where was he?

"David?" She anxiously licked her parched, swollen lips.

Then his mouth was on hers and he was kissing her. Madly. Deeply. Completely. Instinctively, Kelli tilted her hips up, seeking contact with his body, but she found nothing but air.

"Lie still," he commanded softly.

She immediately did as he asked. Then she was rewarded a moment later with the feel of his fingers on the blazing, hungry flesh between her legs, the unmistakable sound of a foil packet being torn open, followed by a deep thrust that found him inside her.

She cried out and reached out to clutch him. Either he had forgotten his command, or he was as out of his mind with pleasure as she was, but he didn't fight her when she clutched his back, pulling him full against her, grinding her hips upward against him.

She didn't think she'd ever feel this kind of excruciating bliss ever again.

Then he began to move in and out of her with long, powerful thrusts and she was proved a liar.

"You feel so damned good," David groaned.

And she was a goner. The world behind her blindfold exploded into a million different colors. David increased the pace of his rhythm, driving deeply into her again and again and again, drawing out her orgasm to unbelievable proportions, until he, too, went rigid and shouted out her name.

It could have been minutes later. It could have been hours. But as Kelli lay there flesh on flesh, flesh in flesh with David, she knew one thing for certain. She'd never be the same woman again.

She felt David shift. "Turn your head," he whispered into her ear. She did so, and he untied the blindfold, slipping it from in front of her eyes. She blinked, finding the room awash in candlelight and the colored lights from the tree. And to find herself painted from neck to toes in black and red paint. He'd traced licking red flames from the tips of her breasts down to the apex of her thighs.

"Merry Christmas, Kell," he murmured, kissing the side of her mouth. "And it's not over yet. Just think...now it's time to do the other side." He withdrew from her, then cupped her womanhood almost roughly in his hand. "Do you have any idea how much you make me want you?"

She reached out and curled her fingers around his already hardening erection. "If it's anything like the way you make me want you, then I think I have a clue."

He groaned, tightened his hand over hers, then gently removed them both. He began to turn her over. Kelli only too willingly helped, reveling in the satiny feel of the fabric and paint against her breasts, then blindly, insatiably thrusting her bottom into the air, longing for him to be back inside her...*now*.

The sharp chirp of ringing sliced through the intoxicating atmosphere. It took two full rings before Kelli realized that it, indeed, was the telephone. To think, somewhere out there beyond the windows, the world continued to turn. It seemed impossible.

"Ignore it," David ordered. He pulled her down on the cushions so that her legs were on either side of his where he knelt behind her.

Then another ringing acted as a shrill counterpoint to the ringing of her phone. She slowly came to understand that it was his cell phone.

David groaned, his hands still against her ankles.

"Ignore it," she told him.

She felt his absence before she saw it, and instantly wanted to pull him closer. She looked over her shoulder to find him fishing his cell phone out of his coat pocket. He closed his eyes and muttered a curse. "Sorry, Kell, I can't. My sister-in-law Mel is on labor watch."

Kelli slowly got up onto her knees, reluctantly dragging the towel to cover herself.

"Hello?" A moment later, David covered the mouthpiece. "It's her. They're taking her to the hospital right now." Into the phone, he said, "You guys have impeccable timing, you know?"

Kelli moved to pick up her own phone, which was on something like its tenth ring. "Hello?"

Her father's voice rang out loud and clear. "What the hell is McCoy doing up there?"

Kelli started and pulled her towel closer, feeling suddenly all too exposed, too vulnerable. "Where are you?" She turned around as if half-expecting to find him in the room.

"Parked on the street."

David hopped into his jeans, then put his boots on. He came up behind her and put his hand over the mouthpiece. "Put your clothes on, you're coming with me."

"Daddy? You and I are going to have to talk about this later. We're going to the hospital."

12

DAVID RUSHED into the hospital waiting room that was filled to the rim with McCoys, then realized he was missing something. Ducking back into the hall, he grasped Kelli's hand then tugged her in along with him.

"David!" Little Lili called, flinging her four-year-old body into his arms.

"Whoa there, Princess," he said, sweeping her up into his embrace. He was aware of a sudden silence as his brothers Connor, Jake and Mitch and his two sisters-in-law Michelle and Liz stared openmouthed at Kelli, but he chose to ignore it. He instead focused on his blond niece, Jake's adopted daughter. She was by far the easiest to deal with. She wouldn't look at him like he'd grown two heads just because he'd brought a woman along with him. "Lili, I'd like you to meet Kelli. Kelli, this is Lili."

"Hi, Kelli," his niece said, bestowing her with one of her urchin grins. Kelli returned the greeting. "Uncle David, you should have seen Aunt Melanie." She cupped her hands over his ears then said in a loud stage whisper, "She said all kinds of bad words in the car that Papa says she shouldn't have said, but that she was hurting real bad, 'cause my cousin is trying really, really hard to come out, and Aunt Liz said it's like trying to fit a watermelon through a mouse hole."

In the corner, Liz reddened, and the rest of them burst out laughing. David looked back down at his niece, tucking strands of her near-white hair behind a tiny ear. "Actually, I like the stork story a little better. Don't you?"

Michelle, Lili's mother, moved to stand before Kelli. "Hello," she said in her nicely Americanized French accent. "My name is Michelle."

"Um, hi," Kelli said, clearly uncomfortable.

"Why don't you come with me, Lili," Michelle said. "You still have that picture to finish for Aunt Melanie."

"Oh, yeah!" The energetic little girl wriggled to be let down. "You think she'll like it?"

Michelle smiled. "Sure, why not? Everyone likes to see a picture of themselves caught at their red-faced worst."

"Speaking of red-faced," Liz got up from where she was sitting and introduced herself to Kelli, as did Connor, Jake and Mitch. David noticed that Pops stayed off to the side, not needing introductions, but not appearing upset by the surprise addition to the group.

Kelli smiled somewhat nervously. "There are so many of you."

David curved his neck to look out into the hall. "And Marc?"

Mitch hooked his thumb toward the window. "I'm surprised you didn't see him when you came in."

David stepped to the wall-long stretch of glass to look outside. Three floors down, Marc's gaze was plastered to the window as he paced about ten feet, then paced back again, his hands thrust into his jeans pockets as light snow swirled around him.

"The expectant father?" Kelli asked softly.

David grinned. "Yeah."

"What's he doing down there?"

"Long story. You see Marc has a bit of trouble with hospitals." David shook his head then turned back toward his family. "Melanie must be fit to be tied."

Connor grimaced. "You don't want to know. Marc will be lucky if she doesn't toss his cowardly butt into the street after all is said and done."

"Ouch."

"Yeah."

KELLI'S MUSCLES were pulled tighter than a towrope. She didn't belong here. Not in this room with this incredibly warm, incredibly *large* family who were sharing a very special time in their lives. She'd known David had four brothers and that three of them had just recently married, but she hadn't thought ahead to when she might actually meet them. Her gaze flicked to where Sean McCoy was awfully quiet in the corner. No, she didn't belong here at all.

She tugged on David's shirtsleeve. "Um, can I talk to you...in the hall?"

He seemed to understand the seriousness of her request. "Sure."

She led the way out as David excused them, then turned as soon as they were out of sight. "I don't belong here," she blurted. "I think...well, don't you think it would be a good idea if I left?"

He skimmed her arm with his hand, reminding her that just underneath her heavy burgundy wool turtleneck sweater and jeans the entire front of her body was covered with body paint. "Kelli, you belong here because I want you here."

"Yeah, but—"

"Kelli Marie, I demand to know what's going on here this very minute."

Kelli's heart leapt up into her throat at the sound of the commanding voice booming down the hall. She didn't have to turn to know that her father must have followed them from her apartment and was even now bearing down on them. She could read it all in David's shocked expression. Could feel it in the dread lining her stomach.

He drew to a halt next to her. "Are you planning on answering me, girl?"

She rolled her eyes toward the ceiling. "David...could you...I mean, would you mind waiting for me in the other room?"

His gaze scanned her face, looking more concerned than she could deal with right now. Finally, he nodded. "I'll be in there. You know, if you need anything."

"What could she possibly need from you, McCoy?"

Kelli planted her palms against David's chest. "Just go. I'll be okay."

He reluctantly did as she asked. As soon as he had rounded the corner, she turned on her father. "How dare you follow me here!"

"How dare I? What did you expect me to do after you tell me you're going to the hospital, then hang up in my ear? Good God, girl, I thought there was something wrong. I spent the past fifteen minutes stalking the emergency room and grilling the nurses there, but no sign of you. Then it occurred to me that since you came with...with that McCoy that it might be something related to him. That's when I found out that one of...them is delivering a baby."

Kelli kept her gaze steady on him. "David's sister-in-law is having the baby, Dad. And it's Sean's first biological grandchild."

His gaze dropped to the floor. "I don't care if Sean himself is giving birth, Kelli."

She curved her hands into tight fists, willing the growing tension in her muscles away. "So then what do you want?"

"I just told you—"

"No, Dad. You explained why you followed me—us—to the hospital. You didn't say anything about what you were doing sitting outside my apartment at ten o'clock at night."

She didn't think it was possible, but his reddened face flushed even further. He mumbled something under his breath.

She crossed her arms over her chest. She nearly had a coronary when her sleeve budged up, revealing the paint there. She tugged at the woolen material, thinking that if she did have a heart attack, at least she'd have a valid reason for being there.

"Dad?"

He expelled a deep breath. "I came to apologize."

Kelli's brows shot up high. "What?" she whispered.

"I said I came to apologize, damn it. Don't act so surprised. It's not like I haven't apologized before, you know."

She nodded stupidly. "Right." She scratched her nose, regarding him cautiously. "Do you want to share exactly what you're apologizing for?"

"For God's sake, can't you figure that one out for yourself?"

She twisted her lips, standing firm.

"All right. I'm apologizing for giving you such hell for...well, you know, getting involved with that McCoy."

"David," she reminded him.

"Yeah, with David."

Kelli was surprised to find that as soon as the words were out, he seemed to relax. "I don't know. After the other night I've been doing a lot of thinking. I would have told you earlier, at your aunt's, but you kept avoiding me and, well, I didn't know quite how to say it. But I think I finally have it all figured out."

He paced a short ways away, then came back again. "All this, this feud with Sean...it's about more than just that we dated the same woman, David's mother. Much more." He violently thrust his fingers through his hair. "Aw, hell, Kelli, I don't know any other way to say this except to just say it. I'm responsible for your mother's death."

Kelli felt all the blood drain from her face. "What?" she whispered.

"Don't look at me that way. I wasn't the one who threw the blow that took her life...but I might as well have been." He dragged a shaking hand through his short-cropped hair then stared at the ceiling. "I don't even know how to put this so it makes some kind of sense." He looked directly at her. "I know it sounds stupid, but...well, in retrospect, doesn't everything?

Even after all those years with your mother, I was still convinced in some juvenile, twisted way that I loved Kathryn Connor, David's mother. And I think your mother knew it. If she didn't know it, she suspected it. Not that she said anything. But I think that's what chased her into another man's arms."

Kelli's mind battled against the information. No. It couldn't be true. She remembered a delicate woman dedicated to her family, nurturing to her daughter, true to her husband. She pressed her fingertips against her temple. "Mom was having an affair when she was killed?" she whispered.

Garth Hatfield looked as though the weight of two worlds rested on his shoulders as he stepped toward a row of connected chairs and collapsed into one. He bent forward, cradling his head in his hands. When he spoke again, it was so softly she had to strain to hear him. "This is all so complicated, Kelli. I think it's why I never said anything, never talked about your mother until now. I always blamed myself, you know? It wasn't until after she was gone that I..." His voice broke and Kelli realized the big strong rock of a policeman that had always been her father was on the verge of breaking down.

She stood frozen to the spot, trying to make sense of what he was saying. Trying to make sense of how she felt about it. She slowly moved to sit next to him and gently put her arm around him.

He looked at her, his face filled with anguish. "It wasn't until after she was gone that I realized how damn much I really loved her. That focusing my attention on a woman I couldn't have was a way to protect myself from getting hurt by another woman. To keep her from leaving me. Ironic that my defense should be the very thing that chased her away."

She drew her hand down his back then up again. Emotionally, Kelli was ill-equipped to handle the upheaval of everything she'd believed was true about her family. About her father, her mother. So it was with a monumental force of will that

she put the personal part of it aside and attempted to focus instead on the facts. If her mother had been having an affair, then
her...lover was a suspect in her murder.

She swallowed hard against the bile rising in her throat.
She'd lived with the facts surrounding her mother's death for
so long that it was altogether difficult to fit the new, shiny piece
into the puzzle. Though once she found the hole, it slid in easily. Her mind raced with the possibilities. Her heart pumped
with the need to follow each and every one of them. To find the
man who had so brutally taken her mother from her. To find
the man who had robbed his father of his wife.

She bit down hard on her bottom lip, then released it.
"Dad...did you know who she was...involved with?"

He shook his head. Though physically he sat right next to
her, his face held a faraway expression as he stared off into a
past she couldn't see. "No. And I never told anyone either." He
fisted the hands resting in his lap. "In fact, I made sure that the
guys at the station, and in homicide, never found out anything
about the affair."

"But why?" she whispered. Doing so would have brought
about a closure Kelli hadn't even dared dream of.

He looked at her pleadingly, the whites of his eyes strained
and red. "Don't you see, Kelli? Even though I couldn't protect
your mother in life, I could in death. It was better for it to have
appeared that she was killed by a random attacker than everyone to know that she was murdered by her lover."

"Oh my God," Kelli whispered, slowly standing up. What
he'd said made a perfect, demented kind of sense.

And turned everything she'd ever believed upside down.

"Oh my God," she said again.

They stayed that way for long minutes, staring at each other,
coming to terms with what had just been revealed.

Garth shakily rose to his feet and moved toward the waiting
room that held what seemed like a ton of McCoy muscle.

"Where are you going?" she asked, panic trying to wriggle through the shock engulfing her.

He looked at her, his face drawn into grim lines, as though he'd lost his wife now instead of eighteen years ago. "I'm going to do what I should have done a very long time ago. I'm going to apologize to the best friend I ever had. I only hope he'll forgive me."

Kelli watched him disappear into the room, her eyes brimming with tears. "He will, Dad," she whispered. "He will."

A SHORT TIME later, David slid his gaze from where Garth Hatfield stood talking to Pops quietly in the corner, to Kelli, who looked more pale than he'd ever seen her. He didn't know what had gone down in the hall, but whatever it was, Garth was talking to Pops and not threatening to take him out back and have at him. He scratched his head, still trying to figure that one out.

He leaned over to Kelli and whispered, "Are you all right?"

She looked a million miles away. Then his words seemed to register and she nodded her head. "I will be."

He began to ask what she meant by that when a resident dressed in blue scrubs poked her head in through the door. "Mr. McCoy?"

All five of the McCoys in the room answered, confusing her.

"Um, we're moving Mrs. McCoy to the delivery room now."

"Thanks," Mitch said. He pulled a cell phone out of an inside jacket pocket and pressed a speed dial number. David looked out the window to see Marc fumbling to answer his. "The time has arrived, Daddy. If you hope to be there for the blessed event, and I highly recommend that you are, then you'll conquer that stupid fear of yours and get up here now."

David could hear Marc shouting over the line before Mitch hit the disconnect button. In the parking lot below, he watched Marc nearly throw his cell phone into a snow bank, then shake his fist at the window. Then he stalked toward the building.

"I'll be damned. I think he's coming."

Connor grumbled. "Don't hold your breath. He's been coming for the past hour. Always chickens out at the last minute."

Jake chuckled. "He'll be lucky if he makes it for the next child born."

David stared at his older brother. This new, chatty, wisecracking Jake was taking some getting used to. Michelle threaded her arm through his and took his hand, reminding David exactly why his brother had changed. He looked at Kelli and smiled, wondering at the changes she'd wrought in him. But given the anxious expression on her face, he didn't think now was the time to bring it up.

"You want to go get some coffee?" he asked instead.

She quickly nodded.

"Okay." His gaze swept the room. "Anybody else want anything?" He committed the large order to memory, then took Kelli's hand and began leading her from the room—only to be nearly mowed down by a frantic Marc.

"Where is she?" he demanded, looking like a caged animal. His gaze darted from wall to wall as if expecting them to close in on him at any second. Liz rushed forward to show him the way.

"Well, I'll be damned," Pops said from the corner.

KELLI WRAPPED her fingers around the steamy foam cup, willing the warmth to seep through to her bones. She'd never felt so cold in her life. It didn't help matters any that she shouldn't even be here. She longed instead to be home where she could slip into bed and pull the covers over her head until the world started making some sort of sense again.

David motioned toward a free table near the corner. "What about the stuff the others wanted?" she asked.

"They can wait a few minutes. I want to talk to you."

She frowned and slid into a chair he held out for her. He took the one across the table. It slowly began to dawn on her that he was acting a tad...odd. Ever since they left the waiting room, he'd looked a little preoccupied. As though he was nervous about something.

She blew on her coffee then took a long sip. "If you're going to ask what's going on between my father and yours—"

He shook his head. "No. Right now that's the last thing on my mind."

She set her cup on the table, though she didn't release it. "Then what is?"

There it was. That anxious expression again. The one that made him look like he was the expectant father rather than his brother Marc. And considering how manic Marc had appeared a few minutes ago, that was saying a whole lot.

He drew in a deep breath and sat back. "This isn't really what I had in mind when I planned to do this," he said softly. "But now that we're here..." He looked at his watch, causing Kelli to do the same. It was eleven-thirty. "Good. It's still officially Christmas."

Kelli grimaced. "David, what are you talking about?"

She watched as he reached into one side of his leather jacket, then the other. "I was supposed to do this after we'd, um, well, you know...at your place...." He extracted something. More specifically, a box. In particular, a ring-sized box. He sat it on the table between them.

Kelli's heart contracted painfully in her chest, making it impossible to breathe. Please...no. She was filled with an instant, incredible urge to run.

David got up and rounded the table. She could do little more than watch him wide-eyed, paralyzed, as he dropped to one knee beside her and placed his hands over hers that were nearly crushing the flimsy coffee cup. "Kelli Marie Hatfield, will you do me the honor of being my wife?"

She heard hushed murmurs from neighboring tables. Felt the leap of her own stomach. The warmth of his hands covering hers. And the undeniable swell of panic rush up into her throat.

She jerked her hands away from his and ran for the door.

"Kelli!" he called after her.

She was almost there.

He caught her arm and hauled her to face him.

She frantically searched his eyes. "What are you crazy, McCoy? I can't marry you." She realized her voice was near a shriek and fought to control it. "For God's sake, I hardly even know you."

His expression moved from confusion, to worry, then amusement. "Not exactly the response I was hoping for."

She shrugged his hand off her arm. "I really can't deal with this right now, David! In fact, with everything going on, I don't know if I'll ever be up to dealing with this. Certainly not tomorrow. Maybe not ever. Don't take it personally, okay?"

She turned and began walking away again, when he hurried past to stop in front of her. "Don't take it personally? Did you really just say that. And just what exactly is that supposed to mean? Of course I'm taking it personally, Kelli. You just essentially ripped my heart out and stomped on it in front of God and everyone. Just how in the hell am I supposed to take it?"

She held up her hand, her head swimming with everything that had happened that night and was continuing to happen. "Everything is...I mean, this is...everything's just moving too fast, David. You're moving too fast."

He grinned. "All right then. So we'll set our wedding date for next year. Two years from now. I don't care."

She stared at him, openmouthed. "Are you paying attention, McCoy? I said I can't deal with this right now. Do you understand?" She began to maneuver her way around him, a sob welling up in her throat. "Why couldn't you just leave things the way they were?"

"Because I couldn't," he said softly, his words halting her more effectively than any physical touch. "I love you, Kelli

Hatfield. And I want to spend the rest of my life with you. Another month together, another six months together, won't make that any clearer for me. In fact, I knew it the first moment I laid eyes on you back at that bar."

She blinked at him, hating him for saying what he was, hating her heart for responding so fully. She quickly erected an invisible defense against him, against his words, no matter how shoddily built the wall. "That's the trouble with you, David McCoy. You're so full of yourself not even you can see past your own ego. You make a decision, see something you want, and you charge in with your battle flag, intent on victory by any means necessary. You always have to be the best. The first man in. The one who saves the day." Her voice cracked. "You have to learn to see that second place doesn't always mean defeat. That every so often you have to step back in order to be the champion. That sometimes being the hero means letting someone else take the lead." Her gaze faltered and she looked down at her hands. "Life is not always about being a hotshot, David."

He looked at her as if he wasn't following her. "I don't get it, Kell. Is it so wrong for me to want you to love me in return? To need you to put me first? Above your assignment? Above the department? Above your damn career?"

"Yes," she murmured through a well of tears. "Yes, it is."

This time when she walked away, he let her.

13

"WHERE'S KELLI?

David had stumbled back to the waiting room on wooden legs, the ring box in his jacket pocket feeling like it weighed a ton. "Hmm?" He turned toward Garth Hatfield. It took him a moment to realize who he was looking at, and his immediate reaction was one of defense.

He forced himself to relax, finding nothing malevolent on the man's granite features as he asked again, "Where's Kelli? She stop off at the little girls' room?"

David looked down, unable to meet his eyes. Funny that, after all this, Garth Hatfield was now talking to him as though he accepted that he and Kelli were a couple. He could have gone without knowing that fate had a perverse sense of humor. "No. She, um, went home."

Garth cleared his throat. "Yeah, well, I had better get going, too." He said something to Sean about meeting for lunch tomorrow, then began to walk away. "Oh, and David? About the other night...I'm sorry, you hear?"

David could do little more than stare at him as Connor came up on his other side. "Apology accepted, Mr. Hatfield. Thanks for stopping by."

Garth frowned at David, then walked from the room. David became all too aware of his older brother hovering at his side, his gaze a little too watchful, a little too probing. "You all right?" he asked.

David blinked at him. "All right? Yeah, I'm fine. Never been better," he said, though he had never felt worse.

Connor's expression told him he wasn't buying a word, but David took advantage of the lapse in conversation and stepped to the corner of the room where Pops was now standing alone. If his gaze was a little intent on Mel's mom, Wilhemenia, who had apparently come in from Maryland and was standing just outside in the hall, David wasn't going to say anything. As he leaned against the wall next to his father, the old saying that misery loved company popped into his mind.

Sean's sigh caught his attention. "You look about as awful as I feel, kid."

David rubbed his hand over his face, the lack of sleep and the strange twist of circumstances catching up to him. "Ditto."

"You and that pretty young Hatfield hit a rough patch?"

David grimaced. "More like we just slammed into a dead end at full throttle." He dropped his hand to his side. "It wasn't pretty."

"What happened?"

"I asked her to marry me." He shrugged. "She said no."

Sean nodded as if what he'd just said made perfect sense. "I see."

The problem was that none of what had just happened made any kind of sense. Yesterday he'd wondered what the perfect Christmas gift would be for Kelli, and he hadn't hesitated when he thought of buying the emerald engagement ring now burning a hole in his pocket. Not even when the jeweler quoted him a price that normally would have sent him stumbling from the store. He wanted Kelli to be his wife. He wanted to propose to her on Christmas so that the day would be doubly special for them both from here on out. It was as simple as that.

Life is not always about being a hotshot, David.

Now what the hell was that supposed to mean? How did his proposing to her translate into his being a hotshot?

Michelle, sitting nearby, must have overheard what he and Pops were talking about because her head snapped in their direction.

Sean leaned closer. "You know, if you want to leave, everybody will probably understand." Pops cleared his throat and nodded to where Michelle was whispering something to Liz, who then grabbed Mitch's arm. David suppressed a groan. In thirty seconds everyone in the room would know what just happened. He didn't think he could deal with that right now.

"Thanks, Pops."

He began to step away when Sean caught his arm. "You know, it might be a good idea if, you know, you stopped off someplace on the way home. See if there's not something salvageable out of that wreck."

David frowned. "No way." He shrugged his shoulders. "I don't know." He sighed. "We'll see."

For the second time that night he walked out of the room and straight into his brother Marc. It was almost unbearable, the huge grin his brother wore. There was no indication of his deathly fear of hospitals, no sign of discomfort, no hint of his intense hatred for all things antiseptic. Instead he looked like a man who had just experienced one of the happiest moments of his life.

"It's a boy!" he shouted.

KELLI WAS completely numb by the time she finally returned home. Emotionally and physically drained. It had taken her half an hour to get a taxi back to her apartment, and the drive had seemed to take forever. The light, flaky snow that had been falling earlier had turned to rain, making the roads treacherous; the clouds and their seeping wetness mirroring the heaviness of her heart and the tears that slipped down her cheeks. Tears lost in the rain when she'd rushed from the cab to her doorway and gotten caught in the downpour. She didn't think she was capable of doing anything more than climbing into the bathtub, drinking the half bottle of cooking sherry she had left in the kitchen, then passing out with a prayer that the world would make more sense somehow when she finally woke up. Say, sometime next year.

She closed and triple bolted the door behind her, then leaned against the cold wood. Breathe, she ordered herself. Just breathe. Because each breath she dragged in took her farther and farther away from the scenes at the hospital. Because each breath brought her nearer to normalcy.

Her voice choked, she realized that same normalcy had been disrupted. "Kojak?" she said softly. The kitchen door was open, which meant he should be around there somewhere. She visually swept the place. Her gaze passed the bulletin board in the corner, then faltered and went back to it. Hadn't she turned it to the D.C. Executioner case before David had showed up? She could have sworn—

The wood behind her back shook as someone knocked on it from the other side. Putting a hand over her erratically beating heart, she stepped away, turned and stared at it. Only after she'd gotten a hold of herself did she lean in and look through the peephole. Nothing. Then a treat skittered from under the door, rolling until it landed almost under the Christmas tree.

Kelli closed her eyes and rested her forehead against the smooth wood. "Go away, David," she murmured.

He didn't say anything.

Kelli sucked in the salty moisture coating her lips. "I'm not going to let you in, so you can just forget about it and go home."

Nothing. Then finally, "I have to talk to you, Kell. I...we can't just leave everything like this. It's driving me crazy."

She laughed humorlessly. "Yeah, well, maybe you now know what it feels like to be me." She turned around and slid to the floor, her back to the door. "I'm sorry I hurt you, but nothing you can say is going to change things."

"Maybe I don't want to change things."

She listlessly swiped at the tears covering her cheeks. "Yeah, right. I'll buy that along with last week's bread."

"I'm serious, Kell." The sound of something running the length of the door sent a shiver skittering down her back. She imagined it was his hand. "Just let me in. I want to make sure you're okay."

"I'm fine. There, are you happy?"

"Okay, then, I want to *see* that you're okay."

"I'll send you a Polaroid first thing tomorrow."

There was a long silence. She didn't fool herself into thinking he had left. That would be too easy. And David never did things the easy way. "Marc and Mel had a boy," he said quietly.

She squeezed her eyes shut. She didn't want to know that. Didn't want to know anything more about David and his large, warm family. Her head was about to explode as it was. "Congratulations," she said softly.

"Your father and mine are going out to lunch tomorrow."

She ignored that one, recognizing the attempts at normal conversation as being straight out of the Metropolitan Police Department's Procedural Handbook, under the heading "How to Deal With a Nut Case."

He lightly hit the door, vibrating the wood and her head along with it. "Damn it, Kelli, why don't you just open the door so we can talk this out like the adults that we are? Your behavior now is nothing if not childish. I asked you a simple question, you gave me a simple answer. That doesn't have to change anything."

You told me you loved me. After what I just learned about my mother...my father...that changes everything.

"David, there was nothing simple about what you asked me at the hospital." She sniffed and ran the heel of her hand over her nose.

"You have got to be the most stubborn woman I've ever met. No. Let's not bring gender into this. You are the most stubborn *person* I've ever met. Now open this door."

She threw her head back to bang it against the door. "And

you're the pushiest! Just go away, David. I need...time. Alone."

She heard him walk away from the door, then back again. He sighed heavily. "Okay."

"Okay?"

"Yeah, okay. I'm leaving. But I'll be back tomorrow, do you hear me? And the day after that. Then the day after that until you agree to talk to me."

She nodded her head, but didn't say anything. Tomorrow seemed so very far away.

"Try to get some sleep, okay?"

She didn't hear anything for a long time, then finally the sound of his footsteps going down the steps echoed through the hall and the aching chambers of her heart. She closed her eyes and sat there, wrapping her pain around herself along with her arms. It hurt her even more to know that she was hurting him, but she didn't know what else she could do right then. Everything she had ever believed about her mother and father had been shattered within a few precious minutes of conversation with her father. Then David's proposal had come from so far out that she responded the only way she knew how: she ran.

She lethargically pushed herself up with the help of the door, peeled off her coat, kicked off her shoes, then dragged herself toward the kitchen.

"You should have let your boyfriend in, Kitty Kat."

Kelli swung toward the voice. Jeremy Price was leaning against the jamb of her bedroom door, regarding her with a wry grin.

It took a full minute for her to register that he was really there. To work out that she hadn't, in fact, let him in. To understand that he must have gained entrance to her apartment some other way. She pushed her damp hair back from her face. "God, Jeremy, you scared the hell out of me." His expression wavered, edging her closer to the precipice leading to all-out fear. She crossed her arms. "How did you get in?"

Removing a hand from his pocket, he held up a set of keys. "A complete copy of the keys you use to let yourself in."

Her throat tightened. He must have swiped her house keys while she was at work and had a copy made at the locksmith's next door to the shop.

Her overworked mind slowly clicked into gear. Her gun. Her gun was in her nightstand table away from where Kojak could get at it and accidentally set it off with his beefy paws and curious nature. And Jeremy was blocking the door to the bedroom.

"So, there's trouble between you and the Casanova Cop, huh? Tsk-tsk. And you two made such a cute little couple." The flagrant effeminate drawl he spoke with now made her realize that up until this moment he'd been talking in an unaffected voice tonight. She followed the realization through again.

"So you know who I am," she asked absently.

He nodded. "Uh-huh. One Kelli Marie Hatfield. Officer Hatfield up until a short time ago. Until you volunteered for a special task force undercover assignment, namely, as a floor girl at my shop."

He stepped away from the doorway, his gait more confident than she'd ever seen it at the shop. She put the fact together with the difference in his speech patterns and realized he wasn't gay at all. Had only pretended to be gay. Likely as a cover-up for other activities. Such as his role as the D.C. Executioner.

She suppressed the urge to nervously rub her neck even as she covertly scanned the apartment for something she could use as a weapon. It was then she saw that all the playtime paraphernalia that she and David had indulged in was still spread out between the sofa and two chairs. And that even now, under her respectable clothes, she was painted nearly head to foot.

He stepped to her bulletin board, still close enough to stop her from making a run for the door. He tapped the board until it rotated to the other side, the side that outlined his own crimes. "You know, I couldn't believe my luck when you first walked into my place. Since you're working the case, you must know that you fit all the major profiles of my victims."

There. He had just as good as admitted he was the Executioner. Adrenaline surged through her veins. Then the reality that she was likely his next victim stopped her blood altogether.

"But it's more than that." He waved a hand toward the ceiling. "It's almost like Fate had intervened, providing me with the one woman who would tie everything up for me."

She squinted at him, trying to make sense out of what he was saying. She shook her head, eyeing the marble candlesticks on the coffee table. "I don't follow you."

He tapped the board so it rotated again, displaying the details of her mother's case. He gazed almost lovingly at the photo of her mother, drawing the tip of his index finger down the studio shot. "You really do look like her, you know. For a second when you first walked into my shop, I thought you were her." He slanted her a disapproving gaze. "But Loretta would never have dressed to look sleazy."

Kelli shuddered.

He shoved his hands in his pockets then turned his back on the board. "I thought I gave myself away the other day. You know, when I spoke of your resemblance. But it was obvious your mind was on something else."

She looked at the bolted door. She'd been thinking about David. About the wonderful night they had spent together.

David.

Could he somehow still be out in the hall? Was it possible that he would come back again tonight?

"Oh, don't worry about C.C." He gave a chilling chuckle. "That's what I call him. You know, short for—"

"Casanova Cop," she said quietly.

"Yes." He flipped his hand in a loose-wristed way and sighed dramatically. "It's much simpler, don't you think, Kitty Kat?" He dropped his hand back to his side. "Anyway, I watched him drive away from your bedroom window. I trust he won't be coming back again soon."

Kelli looked down at her stocking feet and walked a couple of steps then stopped, pretending she was pacing when she was really angling for a better view into her bedroom. If she could reach the nightstand....

She cleared her throat and looked up, finding him overly interested in her movements, as she suspected he would be. "Are you saying you knew my mother, Jeremy?"

His grin was altogether malicious. "Knew her? Oh, yes. In the most biblical of senses, Kitty Kat."

Kelli's stomach churned. "I don't believe you," she whispered.

"Believe what? That your sweet, innocent mother would have broken her marriage vows to your father? Or that she would deign to become involved with a disgusting porn peddler like me?"

She battled back the acidic bile that rushed up her throat. She closed her eyes and tucked her chin toward her chest to ward off the rush. When she opened her eyes again, she had a clear view around the back of the chairs. She spotted Kojak's motionless legs near the corner of the one farthest from her. A sob welled up in her throat.

Jeremy went on. "I wasn't then what I am now, Kelli. I owned a legitimate bookstore then, a small place in Georgetown not far from where your family lived. In fact it was when Loretta came in to buy books for you that we met."

Kelli fought the desire to clap her hands over her ears. She had yet to fully accept what her father had told her earlier. She didn't want to hear that Jeremy was the man with whom her mother had been having an affair. Wasn't ready to face the man who had... She swung toward him. "You're the one who killed her."

The thunderous expression on his face almost made her step back, though ten feet separated them. "I *loved* her."

Anger, pure and strong, washed through her body. Forgetting her plan to zip into the bedroom for the gun there, she stalked instead toward the bulletin board. "You killed her, Jeremy. The evidence is all here." She smacked the board, causing it to vibrate, then pointed to the crime scene photo detailing the bloody blow her mother had taken to the back of the head. "You beat her to death."

He started toward her, appearing suddenly anxious. He stopped just short of touching distance. "Yes, I hit her. What was I supposed to do? She was breaking off our relationship. Said she loved your father. That she wanted to be the kind of mother you deserved. She was *leaving* me."

"So that's why you had to kill her? Because she didn't want to have sex with you anymore?"

"It was more than sex, damn you! It was love." He pressed his fingers to his temples as if pain had just shot through his head. "And I didn't kill her. It was an accident. We were fighting..." He trailed off, then turned and paced a short ways away. "And I had hit her. Once. Twice. She ran for the bathroom. The only door with a lock in your house. Only I got to her first. Then she...then she..." He looked at her. "Then she slipped on something on the bathroom floor. A tub toy. A duck! It was a duck. I couldn't stop her. She fell and hit her head on that old ceramic bathtub. Oh, God, the blood...."

Kelli's heart beat loudly in her ears. She didn't want to hear this from him. Didn't want to hear how her mother had spent her last moments. Didn't want to hear that it may have been her bath toy that had caused her mother to take that fatal fall.

But she *needed* to hear all of it. She'd spent two-thirds of her life needing to hear it.

She had to force the words through her throat. "Okay, Jeremy. I believe you." She swallowed hard. "Even so, how does one go from an accidental death to the types of horrible crimes you're committing now? From depraved sex acts to rape then...murder?"

His gaze cut her to the bone. "I didn't want to do it. I never loved anyone the way I loved your mother. I sought out women who looked just like her but was never able to recreate the same...passion we shared." He whipped his hand back angrily as though lashing out at an unseen something. Kelli winced. "Don't you see? I had to punish her in some way. Had to make her pay for what she had done to me."

"By terrorizing women who resembled her," she whispered.

Jeremy pressed his palms to his temples as if unable to hold everything inside his head. He turned his back to her and paced a couple of steps away. Emboldened by his lack of alertness, Kelli desperately searched the area immediately surrounding her for something she could use as a weapon. Her new vantage point allowed her a full view of Kojak. There were bloodstains on his head and his left back leg. But it was his gentle, almost unconscious panting, the sight of his tongue as it lolled out from the side of his mouth, that made tears collect in her throat.

Oh, Jackie boy.

Spotting the heavy iron lamp on the sideboard next to her, she picked it up, yanking on it to pull the plug from the outlet. It wouldn't give. Hoping the cord was long enough, she raised the heavy lamp above her head then brought it down full force across Jeremy Price's shoulders. She heard the crack of bone, then lifted the lamp to hit him again. But he was quicker than she was. He turned, then charged her. An animal-like yell threatened to break her eardrums as he slammed her against the wall under the entire force of his larger body. The breath rushed from her lungs in a frightening gush and no air quickly followed. She wheezed and dropped to sit on the floor, slumping forward. She was afraid she'd never be able to draw a breath again when finally a small amount of air inflated her lungs.

"You little witch!" Jeremy yelled, hunched over as he picked up the lamp. He hurled it at her, causing the old, frayed, fabric-covered cord to snap, throwing sparks everywhere. Kelli flinched as the base of the lamp landed mere inches away from her leg. She tried to move, but a piercing pain ripped through her rib cage, effectively pinning her in place. She tried to pull in more air and the same pain spread like a thunderbolt through her entire chest. She realized that the impact of hitting the wall must have cracked a rib.

The smell of something burning brought her head up. She looked over to where the still plugged in half of the lamp cord had landed near the paint-smeared fabric David had laid out earlier. Her gaze darted to Jeremy to find him bent over double, trying to assess his own injuries, then back to the makeshift bed. Tiny blue flames licked across the paint-covered surface.

"Oh, God." Tightly holding the side of her rib cage that hurt the worst, Kelli rocked herself to her knees. But every time she drew in air, it felt like fire was burning its way down into her lungs. She leaned forward until her forehead was touching the floor, then fell over onto her side. She blinked, surprised to find the apartment already filling with thick, acrid smoke.

Panic welled in her stomach. She had to get out of there. She tried to bring herself to all fours again. The sound of a low whine filled her ears.

"Where in the hell are you?" Jeremy shouted.

Kelli found she couldn't make him out either, though he was probably no more than ten feet away from her.

Something touched her shoulder and she flinched, until she realized that Kojak had fastened his teeth to the fabric of her turtleneck and was trying to drag her across the room. A sob caught in her throat as she helped him, finding footholds against nearby furniture and propelled herself along the wood floor.

Kojak released her. Kelli looked up to find they were in her bedroom. The smoke wasn't as bad in here. She reached out and drew her hand carefully along the uninjured side of Kojak's face, then realized she was still a bed-length away from the nightstand that held her gun.

With the help of the mattresses, she brought herself to a standing position, every movement sending chilling shards of pain through her chest. She slowly edged her way around the bed, fighting the urge to cough, afraid that if she started she wouldn't be able to stop.

"Oh, no you don't," Jeremy said from behind her.

She swiveled around just as he grabbed her arm and sent her sprawling back in the direction of the door. She hit the door at an angle, slamming it shut as she slipped back down to sit on the floor.

She was never going to make it out alive.

But that had been Jeremy's intention all along, hadn't it? While fire might not have been his preferred weapon of choice, dead was dead no matter which way you cut it.

The windows to his back, Jeremy stood watching her, still slightly slumped over. "What were you going for, Kitty Kat?" He reached behind him and pulled her service revolver out from the waist of his slacks. "Were you looking for this?"

Kelli slid farther toward the floor. Even if she had made it to her nightstand, it would have been for nothing. He'd had her gun all along.

Jeremy ran his hand along the back of his head, then looked at it where it was covered with blood. His breath came in long, ragged gasps. "I had planned to take my time with you, Kitty Kat. Find out if making love with the daughter is as good as with the mother. But you screwed all that up, didn't you?"

"You're the one who started the damn fire, you moron."

Kelli didn't quite know what she had hoped to accomplish by egging him on, but at this point she was beyond caring, beyond playing it safe. If she was going to die, she was going to die having had the last word.

He lifted the gun and pointed it at her.

She held her chin up high. "Go ahead, Jeremy. Shoot me."

In the other room, she heard the whoosh of the fire as it devoured something else. She looked toward the windows, even now trying to figure a way out of the mess. She noticed that the one to the right was halfway open. It was also the reason there wasn't much smoke in the room. The bulk of it billowed out into the rainy, frigid night air.

She swung her gaze back to Jeremy. "What's the matter? So long as you can beat a woman into submission, rape her, you're A-number one. Macho sick-o of the year. But put a gun in your hand and you turn into an impotent wimp."

"Impotent?" he cried. "Impotent?"

Something behind Jeremy moved. Not something, she realized, but someone. Hope poured over Kelli as surely as the rain had a short while ago.

David.

When she'd refused to let him in the apartment, he must have climbed up her fire escape, determined to gain entrance that way.

God bless his pushy, hotshot heart.

Jeremy squeezed off a round just as David slammed his arm hard down on Jeremy's. The bullet hit the wall a foot away from Kelli, spitting plaster against her turned away face.

"You heard the lady," David said, pulling on Jeremy's shoulders and yanking him back against his raised knee. "Impotent."

He easily twisted the gun out of Jeremy's hand, then stepped away from him.

For long moments Kelli concentrated strictly on breathing in and out with as little movement as possible, gazing at David like the knight in shining armor that he was. Then he grinned at her.

"I'm still not all that clear on what you meant by the second place stuff you said at the hospital," he told her quietly. "But...catch, Hatfield."

He tossed the gun in her direction. She held out both hands in her lap and it landed in them cleanly.

She jerked her head up, finding Jeremy coughing up blood and regaining his bearings even as David crossed his arms and backed away. "Do what you have to, Kell," he told her. "I'll back you up one hundred percent."

Kelli fumbled with the gun, then lifted it, setting her sights straight for Jeremy's heartless chest. At the last minute, she lowered her aim and shot him in the knee.

KELLI HAD THREE broken ribs, one of which had punctured her left lung, laying her up in the hospital. Still, her physical injuries couldn't come close to the pain caused by her emotional distress.

She turned her head on the pillow and looked toward the window. Outside the rain had moved on and the sun was beginning to set. She didn't know what kind of pain pills they'd given her but they had knocked her out cold for hours. It was hard to believe that almost a full day had passed since David had carried first her, then Kojak, out to the fire escape, where they had waited until help arrived. Harder still to believe that Jeremy Price was behind bars, likely facing life imprisonment for his actions as the D.C. Executioner.

Kelli looked down at the unappealing green of her hospital gown. Nowhere in the reports she'd given had she said anything about Jeremy's connection to her mother. And the fire had effectively burned all evidence that she'd been secretly working on the case. She hadn't even told her father about Jeremy...yet. She was sure she would, eventually. But he was in bad enough shape knowing she had been targeted by the D.C.

Executioner. Anyway, right now *she* was having a hard enough time coming to terms with everything. Coming to terms with the huge mistake she had made in pushing one dashing Casanova Cop away when he had offered her the world.

Groaning, she swiped at her damp cheeks. She'd never cried so damn much in her life as she had in the past twenty hours. You would think she'd be dehydrated by now. Long cried out. But no. Every time she thought of David slipping that ring box out of his jacket pocket...remembered him standing outside her apartment door...recalled spotting him behind Jeremy at the moment she needed him most, her eyes began leaking all over again.

She'd spent the entirety of her adult life trying to solve the mystery of her mother's death. Striving to be the best cop she could be. Yearning for that detective's badge that would allow her to prevent others from suffering as she had since she was seven.

And now that her mother's murderer had been caught? Now that all the mysteries she had been obsessed with were solved?

Well, now she realized she wasn't any more ready for that detective's badge than it was ready for her.

Oh, the time would come. She was sure of that. Catching the D.C. Degenerate-Executioner wouldn't look bad on her résumé, either. But she no longer felt the desire to let her career ambitions rule her life.

No.

Instead, every time she closed her eyes, she saw David. Dear, sweet, exasperating, pushy, sexy David. Which was the only place she saw him because he'd disappeared right after they'd been brought down from the fire escape last night.

She didn't particularly appreciate the irony of the situation. When she'd wanted him to disappear, he'd stuck like glue, not giving up until he got her to give in. Now that she wanted him there, he was nowhere to be found.

The door opened. Kelli hopefully turned her head toward it, then sighed when a nurse entered.

"Good, you're up."

Kelli frowned at her as she kept the door open with one hip, then reached out into the hall. She wheeled what looked like a...was that a baby buggy? With much pain and effort, she lifted herself up onto her elbows.

"Nurse, I think you have the wrong room."

The woman eyed her. "You're Kelli Hatfield, aren't you?"

"Yes, but—"

"Then trust me, this is the right room." Ignoring her protests, she turned the buggy around. Kelli looked down but could see nothing but a large, bulky blue blanket. The nurse smiled at her. "This is breaking every last hospital rule, and could cost me my job if my supervisor found out, but...let it never be said I can't be swayed by a terrific grin and a great pair of buns."

Kelli stared at her, wondering how much medication *she'd* had.

"Are you ready?"

"Ready for what?"

The nurse swept back the blanket. Kelli's eyes opened wide as Kojak gave a plaintive bark, his short tail going a million miles a minute.

"Oh, baby!" At risk of pulling the fifteen stitches in her side, Kelli kicked her own blanket off and put her feet over the side of the bed. Through her tears, she scanned her canine hero from the tips of his ears to his back paws. His sweet little head was swathed in bandages but it didn't keep his juicy tongue from lolling out as he panted happily. But it was the splint on his back leg that concerned her most and was obviously what kept him still when he'd otherwise be loping about looking for treats. She ran her hand down the length of him, laughing with joy when he lapped enthusiastically at her hand.

"But how did you...I mean, who asked you...?" She looked

up to find the nurse was gone and that in her place stood one very handsome, grinning David McCoy.

"I won't even tell you what the vet bill looks like," he said, standing with his hands stuffed into the pockets of his jeans, his black leather jacked unzipped to reveal a soft red, chambray shirt. "It wasn't pretty. And we won't even talk about your apartment."

Kelli's smile widened so far it nearly hurt her face. "Well, it's a good thing you two are a sight for sore eyes, then, isn't it?"

"Not to mention broken ribs." He glanced toward where her hospital gown was bunched up around her thighs. "How are you, um, doing?"

"Aside from feeling like I just got run over by a train? Fine." She continued patting Kojak. "I, um, can't thank you enough for this. I was just lying here feeling lonely and sorry for myself. Kojak...and you were just what the doctor ordered."

"Me?"

She held up the hand she'd been using to pet Kojak. "Before you start, McCoy, there are a few things I'd like to say."

His grin slipped. "If it's something I've already heard before, don't bother."

She shook her head and leaned back on her hands to take the pressure off her ribs. "Trust me, this is probably the last thing you're planning to hear."

His brows budged up on his handsome forehead. "Well, then, please, don't let me stop you."

She laughed, then groaned when pain shot through her chest. "Oh, please, don't make me laugh."

He stepped closer to her, helping her to lie back down. His touch was meant to be helpful, nurse-like, but she was coming to learn that the most innocuous of touches from him set her body on fire. If she was in any kind of shape to, she'd have pulled him down on top of her right that minute and prayed no one walked in while she molested him.

"So..." he prompted.

She rolled her eyes toward the ceiling. "You can't even wait for a lady to catch her breath, can you? Pushy 'til the end."

He brushed her hair back from her face. The sensitive gesture sent her eyes back to watering.

"Kell?" he said softly. "We can talk about this later if you want to."

She gave him a watery smile. "Now he wants to talk later." She caught her bottom lip between her teeth. "All I wanted to say is that...well, what I mean is...oh, hell." She gathered up her courage, then blurted, "Yes."

His grimace was so endearing she wanted to laugh, but didn't dare. "Yes?" he said, puzzled. She narrowed her eyes. "Yes," he repeated again, apparently searching his mind for the question. She knew the instant it hit him because his blue, blue eyes virtually shot sparks, and his face lit up like the Christmas tree on the White House lawn. "Yes!"

His kiss was wonderful and wet and hot and sent her senses spiraling. She moaned when he pulled away.

"I, um, do have a condition, though," she said softly.

"Name it. Whatever it is, I'll live with it without pestering you. I promise."

"I need some time to get used to the idea. That means we don't get married right away."

His gaze was weighty as he looked at her. "That's okay. I meant what I said last night, Kelli. Next month, next year. It's all the same to me. Just so long as I know that eventually you'll be my wife." He waggled his eyebrows at her. "We are going to live in sin, though, aren't we?"

She laughed before she could stop herself, then coughed from the pain. "No, we are not going to live in sin. You think my father was bad before, let him get wind of you even suggesting such a thing and I'll be a widow before I'm a bride."

"So where are you going to live then? I mean, you can't exactly go back to your apartment. I'm sorry to be the one to tell you this, Kell, but there's nothing there to go back to."

That left her father. She cringed. Or Bronte, who had called that morning to say she was catching the first flight back into town to see her. Still... "Maybe this living in sin thing isn't such a bad idea. And we can always get married in the spring."

"Spring? As in next year?"

She hit him in the arm. "As in this year, silly. Three months away." She closed her eyes and smiled. "When the cherry blossoms are blossoming. There's something about cherries that will probably always make me think of you."

He gently slanted his mouth across hers and she languidly returned his kiss. "Does this mean you love me, Kelli Hatfield?"

She sighed and searched his eyes. "I always thought I liked working...living solo, you know? But after you... Well, all work and no play make Kelli a very dull girl."

"There's not one thing dull about you, sweetheart. Not a single thing." He drew the tip of his nose down her cheek then over to her ear. "But you didn't answer my question, Kell."

She closed her eyes and turned her face so it lay against his, breathing in everything that was him. "I love you, David McCoy. More than the air that I almost breathe."

There was a hesitant knock at the door. Kelli ignored it as she threaded her fingers through his thick blond hair, holding him against her. He shifted his head then a quiet chuckle vibrated his chest. She pulled back to gaze at him.

"Looks like you have visitors," he said.

Kelli's heart skipped a beat as she looked toward the door. Through the long, narrow window stood not one, not two, but all five of the other McCoy men and two of the McCoy women, along with a sheepish-looking Garth Hatfield. She managed a shaky smile, then lifted a hand to wave at them.

David got up off the bed and swung the door open. "We're getting married," he blurted.

But rather than letting his and her family in as she suspected he would, he closed the door in their shocked faces, yanked the privacy panel to conceal them from view, then carefully climbed into the narrow bed next to her.

"Now...where were we?" he asked, grinning that naughty grin that made her want to surrender to him completely. It was pure heaven to finally let herself....

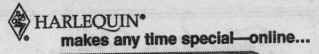

INDULGE IN A QUIET MOMENT
WITH HARLEQUIN

Get a FREE
Quiet Moments Bath Spa

with just two proofs of purchase from
any of our four special collector's editions in May.

Harlequin® is sure to make your time special this Mother's Day
with four special collector's editions featuring a short story
PLUS a complete novel packaged together in one volume!

Collection #1 Intrigue abounds in a collection featuring *New York Times*
bestselling author Barbara Delinsky and Kelsey Roberts.

Collection #2 Relationships? Weddings? Children? = *New York Times*
bestselling author Debbie Macomber and Tara Taylor Quinn
at their best!

Collection #3 Escape to the past with *New York Times* bestselling author
Heather Graham and Gayle Wilson.

Collection #4 Go West! With *New York Times* bestselling author
Joan Johnston and Vicki Lewis Thompson!

Plus Special Consumer Campaign!

Each of these four collector's editions will feature a
"FREE QUIET MOMENTS BATH SPA" offer.
See inside book in May for details.

Only from
HARLEQUIN®
Makes any time special ®

Don't miss out! Look for this exciting promotion on sale in May 2001,
at your favorite retail outlet.

Visit us at www.eHarlequin.com   PHNCP01

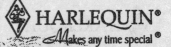